REVENGE

OF THE HAPPY CAMPERS

Don't miss any adventures with The Brewster Triplets!

Revenge of the Flower Girls
Revenge of the Angels

REVENGE

OF THE HAPPY CAMPERS

JENNIFER ZIEGLER

 SCHOLASTIC PRESS / NEW YORK

TO DAD,
FOR THE MEMORIES WE MADE AND
CHARACTER WE BUILT AT PAPPY
CAMP

ISBN 978-1-338-09119-9 • 10 9 8 7 6 5 4 3 2 1   17 18 19 20 21 • Printed in the U.S.A.   23 • First edition, May 2017 • Book design by Yaffa Jaskoll

Dear Mom and Dad,

I hate camping.

Why are you making me do this? Don't I get a vote in what happens to me? This is tyranny at its worst.

You tell me I should love camping because I'm a history buff, and that I should find it interesting to get away from modern society for a while. Well, it's true that camping is like traveling back in time, but to a very boring place.

And not just boring — dangerous!

I'm sending you this email before we leave so that there will be official documentation — and because there won't be wifi or computers where we're going.

So once again, allow me to make my position clear — I HATE CAMPING!

Your oppressed daughter,

Dawn

CHAPTER ONE

Dawn's Early Light

Dawn

Maybe if Darby hadn't been so foolhardy, our camping trip wouldn't have turned into a disaster. The thing was, I knew we'd end up in a real predicament. That very notion woke me up our first morning at the campsite.

It was so early the sun wasn't even up yet. I know because I peeked out the window of our pop-up trailer and could see only a tiny bit of light in the distance, turning the charcoal sky a dark blue color. It seemed like the whole world was sleeping.

I carefully climbed over Darby, slid off the bunk we shared, and tiptoed over to where Delaney slept. Her blankets were all tangled up and her feet were on her pillow, so it took a while to figure out where her head was. I pulled back the sheet and poked her shoulder. "Are you up?" I asked. I had to say it loud enough to be heard over Aunt Jane's snores, but not so loud that it would wake everyone.

Delaney's eyes fluttered. She mumbled, "Chicken," and turned onto her side, away from me. Delaney talks a lot, even in her sleep. But her sleep talking usually doesn't make any sense at all.

"Delaney?" I said a little louder. She didn't move. It's strange watching Delaney be quiet and still, because normally she's a loud blur.

I tried putting my hand on her shoulder and shaking it a little.

"Put it in the chicken," Delaney muttered, and rolled over even farther so that her nose pointed down into the bench cushion.

I sighed and stamped my foot, making the whole trailer tremble slightly. Then I cupped my hands over my mouth and whisper-yelled "Delaney!" right into her ear.

She sat up immediately, her head bonking my chin. "What's going on?" she asked, looking all around her.

"*Shhh!* Follow me," I said. "And be quiet. We don't want to wake up the others."

We tiptoed to the door of the camper, unlatched it, and stepped outside as silently as possible. It was chilly, and the gravel underneath my bare feet was sharp and pointy in places. Slowly we made our way over to the concrete slab where the picnic table stood. I sat on one of the benches, while she stayed standing, staring off into the distance.

"It's hardly even light out yet," Delaney said as she blinked toward the horizon. "Do you feel okay, Dawn? You haven't been the first one up since the day we were born."

My sisters tell me that if I want to be president of the United States, I'll have to learn how to get up early. I say that's no problem, because when something important is happening, I do get up early — without being grouchy. And when you are president, every day you have something important to deal with.

Just like today. Today I was dealing with something important.

"Why are we out here?" Delaney asked.

"I'm calling an emergency meeting," I said.

"But we forgot Darby."

I shook my head. "No, we didn't. I left her out on purpose. She's the reason we're having the emergency meeting."

"Is this because of what happened right after we arrived?" she asked.

"No," I replied. But I could tell by the way her eyebrows became high half circles that Delaney didn't believe me. "We need to have a plan of action. A way to avoid more calamities. While we're here, Darby's going to come up with all sorts of harebrained schemes. And whenever that happens, we always get mixed up in it. You know how she is. If we don't take preventative measures, she'll end up getting us killed. Mom will never forgive us."

"But what can we do?" Delaney asked. She had started

jumping off the other concrete bench of the picnic table, over and over, watching her nightgown flare out as she did it.

"We need to get the details down," I said. "Like we always do."

"But Darby usually types up the notes. And we don't have a computer. Or Darby."

I let out a growl-sigh. I know it isn't fair of me, but sometimes I find the facts of a situation annoying.

"Fine," I said. "How about I review recent events out loud and you bear witness. If anything seems wrong, you can tell me."

"Okay. That's probably best anyway. We aren't going to want to vote on these meeting minutes and file them away. Not if you don't want Darby to see them."

"Now, if you are going to listen and corroborate the facts, you have to stay relatively still. You can bounce and change positions, but no twirling or jumping, okay?"

"Fine," she said, sounding all droopy.

"All right. Here goes." I cleared my throat and made the following official statement:

> Yesterday at approximately 1800 hours, the four of us —
> Darby, Delaney, Aunt Jane, and I — arrived at Lake
> Lewis after driving for four straight hours in the van.

"That was only four hours? It felt like four thousand."

"Delaney, you have to be quiet and bear witness."

Let the record state that we shouldn't even be here. It's spring break of our sixth grade school year and three weeks ago Mom told us Aunt Jane was coming to Texas to visit. This made us go yippee because Aunt Jane is just about our favorite person in the world — only we found out that because Mom was busy with tax season, Dad was going to a work conference, and Lily's spring break wasn't until the next week, Aunt Jane was mainly coming to babysit us.

We are almost twelve years old and don't need a babysitter. But apparently our family is afraid that if we are left unsupervised for long stretches, there will be shenanigans.

"That's probably because of what happened at the —"
"Delaney! Just bear witness."
"Okay. Sorry."

So Aunt Jane decided to take us to Lake Lewis — where she and Mom used to camp all the time while growing up. We'd never been to the lake, but she promised it would be great. Besides, our parents were making us go.

Thus and ergo, we came. And as soon as we arrived and set up the camper, Darby got a wild look in her eye and set off exploring. Delaney and I went after her. For a while, we lost her, and then we heard her calling to us. She told us she'd found the most amazing thing and we had to come see it. Like dummies, we followed.

Darby took us down to the creek. To our right, it disappeared around a bend. To our left, way in the distance, was a wooden bridge, but there didn't seem to be anything but rocks on the other side. And all I saw in front of us were weeds and stinky water. "What's so amazing?" I asked. That's when she pointed to a rope hanging from the bough of a live oak. "Watch," she said. Then she jumped on the rope, swung way out over the water, came back, and jumped off. Her eyes were all gleamy and she had a huge smile on her face. That's when she held the rope out to me.

Let the record also state that she said, and I quote, "I *promise* you'll love it."

It looked so simple when she did it, and I figured it had to be easy. But I was duped. It was *not* fun and I did *not* love it.

"You were screeching like a barn owl."
"Ding-dang it, Delaney! For the last time —"

"I know, I know. Just bear witness."

> We can skim over the exact details, but in summary,
> the rope hurt, the swing took me way out farther and
> higher than I'd expected, I didn't have enough momen-
> tum to get back, I tried to shift positions, I lost my
> grip, and I fell into the water below. The water was
> warm and mossy and stinky because the campground
> hadn't had real rain in a long time. Now one of the
> three outfits I packed is all wet and the only shoes I
> brought are squishy.

At this point Delaney started laughing. I glared at her until she stopped.

Okay, so maybe I *was* still steamed about what happened. But that was beside the point.

"That's pretty much my whole statement," I said. "Now that we've reviewed the facts, we need to come up with a plan."

"For what?" Delaney asked.

Sometimes it's difficult to believe Delaney has an exact copy of my DNA. "For Darby!" I said. "We need to make sure she doesn't lead us down a path of senseless and risky behavior."

"How are we going to do that?" Delaney was twirling again — which annoyed me. As did the absence of worry in her tone. The whole point of getting up early was to solve this problem.

Only I didn't have any ideas, either. I was tired and peevish and still reeked a bit of stagnant creek water. So I was just about to table the discussion for a future emergency meeting when we heard noises.

First there came a creaking sound, followed by the bang of a door. After that came footsteps crunching on gravel, the rustling of people moving through bushes, and, eventually, silence.

Then, out of the darkness, we heard a voice say, "I call this meeting to order."

CHAPTER TWO

Space Race

Darby

That first morning at the campsite, I woke up with Dawn and Delaney shaking me and saying that we'd been infiltrated. It took me a moment to remember where I was and realize I wasn't dreaming.

"Get dressed!" Dawn said, pushing clothes at me. "We have to do surveillance!"

"There's a meeting. Only it's not our meeting. Our meeting is finished. I mean we didn't have a meeting," Delaney was babbling.

Over the years, I've learned to just do what they say. If it had been one sister, I might have asked a lot of questions. But when it's both, I figure I'll be safe just going along with them. At least, probably.

So even with my brain still half asleep and the trailer all cramped and crowded, I managed to put on my shorts and shirt and shoes — and none of them were inside out or backward. Plus, we didn't wake up Aunt Jane, which was amazing.

I followed Dawn and Delaney out of the camper, and Dawn put her finger against her lips to signal that we had to be super silent. Then the three of us crept toward a clump of trees near the picnic table.

As we came closer, muffled voices grew louder. I heard a boy's voice saying, "You mean you already got into the provisions? Why?" followed by another's voice saying, "I couldn't help it. I was hungry."

We got to the grove of oaks and mesquites and carefully picked our way through it for several yards. When we got to the last part of the brambles, Dawn motioned that we should all stop walking and hunker down.

At first, I couldn't see anything. The sky was slowly filling with a pink light, but there were still lots of shadows. And my eyes were all blurry with sleep. Eventually, I could make out shapes and slight movement through the branches.

There were three boys — all different shapes, heights, and colors. The tallest one looked around thirteen. He was skinnier than the other boys and his black hair was curly. The medium-height boy seemed like he was our age. His dark hair was straight and he was a rounder shape than the tallest boy. I guessed the third boy, who was the shortest of all, to be around nine or ten. He had red hair — not gold-red like ours, but red like my red-orange crayon. It glowed like fire in the sunrise.

The tallest boy was the one talking. "In approximately one and a quarter hours we will have breakfast. The food we brought is for scheduled meals only. If you get hungry between meals, you have to eat off the land."

"Eat off the land?" repeated the boy with bright red hair. "How?"

"By looking for berries," the tallest boy replied. "Or catching fish."

"Fish is grody," the red-headed boy said, making a face. "What if I hunted and roasted a rabbit?"

Delaney let out a huge gasping sound, lost her balance, and fell forward, snapping a few twigs on her way down. Dawn and I froze like worried statues.

"What was that?" asked the tallest boy.

"I think it came from over there," said the medium-tall boy, pointing in our direction.

I groaned. We should have realized Delaney would be incapable of staying still and quiet.

"Think it's a wild animal? Should I go get my bow and arrow?" asked the shortest boy.

Dawn and I exchanged scared looks. "Nope! Not wild animals," she called out. She held her hands up in surrender and stepped forward through the brush into the clearing where the boys stood. "It's just us."

Delaney scrambled back onto her feet and pushed past Dawn. "And speaking of animals, you really shouldn't eat rabbits. They're fluffy and bouncy and cute and don't hurt anyone — which means it wouldn't be a fair fight. I have a pet rabbit named Mynah and she's the sweetest ever, so I should know."

For a moment, the boys just stood there, blinking at Dawn and Delaney.

"Um . . . who are you?" asked the tallest boy.

"I'm Delaney. This is Dawn and . . . Darby's around here somewhere. Oh! Over there, trying to hide behind that bush."

I let out another annoyed groan.

See, I'm shy around people — especially people I don't know. And now these guys knew I was trying to hide from them, which made me feel even more bashful.

When Delaney pointed me out like that, I wanted to run back to the trailer and duck back under the covers. Or climb a tree. Or disappear in a puff of smoke like a genie. But I don't want to be shy anymore. Someday I want to be chief justice of the United States Supreme Court. And to do that, I have to be able to look people in the eye — even people I don't know.

So I took a deep breath and waited until I didn't want to run away. Then I stepped out from behind the bush and stood right behind Delaney, hiding only a little bit.

"Are you triplets?" asked the medium-height boy.

"Yeah," Dawn said.

"How'd you get to be that way?" the short, red-headed boy asked. He took a cautious step forward and kept looking back and forth, from me to Delaney.

Delaney shrugged. "We were just born that way."

"And who are you guys?" Dawn asked.

The tallest boy put a hand on his chest. "I'm Jayden. But everyone calls me Jay. This is Roberto." He pointed to the boy around our age, who was standing behind him.

"Everyone calls me Robbie," said Robbie.

"And this is Nelson," Jay gestured to the red-haired boy.

"What do people call you?" Delaney asked.

"Nelson," he said. He looked at us, rubbing his chin as if he had a beard — which he didn't. "So how come you guys are trespassing and spying on us?"

"Hold up there, mister. We might have been spying, but we weren't trespassing," Dawn said, putting her hands on her hips. "This is part of our campsite."

"No, this area is part of our campsite." Jay shook his head fast, making his hair bounce.

"Uh, no," Dawn countered. "As I said, this is our site. We heard you encroaching and had every right to investigate."

"Like I said, this is our area," Jay said. "You are the ones encroaching."

"Oh yeah?" Dawn said. "Prove it."

We all looked around to see if there were markers indicating where one campsite ended and the other began, but we couldn't find anything. By now the sky was full of a thin white light — like stretched-out tissue. Birds were starting to wake up and sing.

We all reassembled back near our original spots and stood there, not knowing what to say.

"Obviously, we need to come up with an understanding," I said. Only I said it softly and Delaney had to repeat it.

"Like what?" Nelson asked.

"How about we divide the area in half?" Dawn suggested.

"Or we can share it," I said.

"Maybe we can all agree that the area belongs to both campsites," Robbie suggested. "Like a neutral zone."

"Yeah! And we can take turns. Like . . . we can have it from midnight to noon and you can have it from noon to midnight," Delaney said.

Jay did his fast headshake again. "No, we should have it in the morning," he said. "We like to get up early."

"You mean *you* do," Robbie mumbled, but I wasn't sure if Jay heard him.

"Yeah, why are you guys up so early?" Delaney asked.

"We were having a meeting," Jay said. "It's just how we do things. You wouldn't understand."

Dawn put her hands on her hips again. "And why wouldn't we?"

Then Jay said something that made Dawn's eyes go wider than I've ever seen them go.

"It's like . . . practice," he said. "For a cabinet meeting. Because someday I'm going to be president of the United States."

CHAPTER THREE

Civil Liberties

Delaney

We picked our way through the clump of trees, heading back to our camp. Daylight was everywhere now. Birds were singing and a breeze was making the leaves dance on the branches. It was the best part of the day — light and cool and cheerful.

Dawn had that fierce look on her face. The one she gets when her brain is all fired up over some injustice. It happens pretty regularly. Last month she had that look and we ended up spending a whole weekend writing letters to the manager of our dad's apartment complex pointing out that their staff should have Presidents' Day off. At first Darby didn't want to waste her Saturday and Sunday writing letters, but I convinced her. I told her that if she helped us with Dawn's letter campaign, we'd help her try to convince Mom to buy a trampoline — so she agreed. I felt proud of myself, since this is just the sort of deal-making I'll have to do when I grow up to be Speaker of the U.S. House of Representatives.

Dawn was grumbling under her breath as she walked to our campsite, and the sound blended in with all the birds that were chirping and twittering around us. I could only make out the words "bigheaded" and "arrogant" and "lousy amateur."

"Dawn? Are you mad because Jay wants to be president?" I asked.

Dawn spun around and shot her fierce expression right at me. "No!" she snapped.

Darby and I exchanged a look. We could tell that Dawn's "No" meant "Yes," and that she was sore at Jay but too stubborn to admit it. I know it seems impossible to communicate all that in a one-second glance, but my sisters and I do it all the time. It's a triplet thing.

"You know, since presidents are elected every four years, both of you could end up being president at some point," Darby pointed out.

You can always count on Darby to be positive and try to cheer people up. Dawn is stubborn, though. Once she's in a bad mood, she usually refuses to budge.

"First of all," Dawn said, kind of huffy-sounding, "the office of the president isn't a carnival ride where everyone takes turns. Secondly, I plan to be reelected and serve at least eight years. They might even change the rules for me to allow a third term. You never know."

"Well . . . you could be president first and then Jay could get elected after you," Darby said.

Dawn shook her head. "And have him tear down all my programs and bad-mouth everything I worked hard to create? Forget it."

"Maybe you could be president after him," I suggested.

"And have him beat me to it? Have him create such a mess of things that I'd have to spend my entire term fixing it? No, thank you."

See what I mean? Sometimes Dawn is just determined to be miserable.

"Well, there's no point in fretting," Darby said. "This is a big campground and we don't have to see those guys anymore. They're probably with a scout troop and will be busy doing their own thing."

Also see what I mean? No matter what, Darby is determined to look on the bright side.

We pushed through the last branches in the brushy section separating the two campsites and saw Aunt Jane standing in front of our little Coleman stove that she'd set on the picnic table. She was already dressed in cropped pants and a striped T-shirt, but her short brown hair was sticking out in all directions so you could tell she hadn't been up long.

"Good morning, girls," she said, waving a spatula at us. "I was just about to make breakfast. Who's hungry?"

"I am! Me! I'm starving!" I said and ran over to her. As soon as she mentioned food, I could feel how empty my stomach was. We'd all been so busy helping Dawn after her plummet into the creek yesterday evening that I never went back for a second hot dog like I'd planned to.

Aunt Jane showed us how to get the stove going and pulled out a big cast-iron skillet. Then she cooked up Spam and eggs. My job was to cut the Spam into little chunks. This made me really happy because at home Mom doesn't like to have me around knives. She says I'm too wiggly and might accidentally chop off a finger. Also, Mom doesn't let us eat Spam at home. Or dinners that come in boxes. Or the kinds of cereal that have prizes in them. But Aunt Jane likes fun food that's easy to make. Once she even let us have pie before dinner!

I was really careful cutting the Spam so that Mom would get a good report from Aunt Jane. Meanwhile, Darby cracked open and beat the eggs, and Dawn cleared off and set the table. She was obviously still miffed about Jay, because she banged down the plates and plastic juice cups and muttered the whole time.

I concentrated really hard and did the cutting perfectly. Only . . . when I was done and bounced around shouting hooray, I accidentally knocked over a cup of juice that ran all over the picnic table. I wiped it up, but the ants, flies, gnats, and bees were congregating around the big wet spot, so Aunt Jane said we should eat in the camper. This made Dawn even more cantankerous.

Luckily, with everyone pitching in, we sat down to eat in a

matter of minutes. Aunt Jane had even picked some nearby wildflowers and put them inside an empty soda bottle with some water. When she set it in the middle of the table, it made the place seem extra snug and homey. Well . . . as homey as an old camper can be.

Our pop-up trailer hadn't been used since our parents divorced, so it's kind of musty smelling (and Dawn's moldy creek-water clothes didn't help). Plus, it must have gone all off-kilter while it was cooped up in Mom's shed for two years, because it tilts a little to one side. Our breakfast dishes kept slowly sliding away from us as we ate.

"You know, I was concerned when I woke up this morning and couldn't see you guys," Aunt Jane said. She turned her head and looked at each of us. Her eyes didn't have that usual twinkle, so it made me squirm and feel guilty. "You should have left a note. You know the rules."

"We're sorry," Darby said. "We . . ." She glanced over at me and Dawn. I could tell she wasn't sure how to explain.

"It was kind of a mission, only we didn't know it was a mission," I said. "Or maybe it was a quest. Or a hunt. But not like a hunt where you kill things. I don't know why someone would ever hunt rabbits." I was blathering and I knew it. I just wasn't sure what to say — and I especially didn't want Darby to know that Dawn had called a secret meeting without her.

"Basically we heard something and went to investigate,"

Dawn said. "And anyway, we're on vacation. I thought we were leaving rules and schedules behind."

"Of course you still have to follow the same rules you have at home," Aunt Jane said.

Darby nodded. "Without rules, we would have anarchy. There have to be rules in order to have civilized society."

"But we're not in civilization. We're camping!" Dawn pointed out.

"Your mom and I had to follow them when we went on our campouts," Aunt Jane said.

This made us sit up to listen. The fact that they had to abide these rules made it seem more right and just. Plus, we love it when she talks about growing up. Sometimes she acts out scenes, with funny voices and everything.

"You're free to wander around, just follow common sense," Aunt Jane said. "Don't go looking for trouble. No poking wasps' nests with a stick or things like that."

"That's crazy. Who would do such a thing?" I asked.

Aunt Jane looked a little shrunken. "It's been known to happen." She reached over and mussed up Dawn's hair — in a nice way — making it almost as unruly as her own. "Listen, I'm being trusted by your parents to look out for you, and I plan to do a good job. I still want you to have fun. In fact, that should be a rule. Have fun — that's an order."

"Can we also add 'No raisins allowed'?" Darby asked. She hates raisins. On the drive to the campsite she found some in the trail mix we were snacking on and drank three boxes of juice to get the taste out of her mouth. We had to make a lot of restroom stops after that.

"No problem," Aunt Jane said. Then she cupped her hands around her mouth and declared loudly, "All raisins and raisin-containing products are hereby outlawed from camp!"

By this time we were done with breakfast, so we all tossed out rules as we gathered up the dishes and took them outside to wash in a plastic bin full of soapy water.

"Chocolate every day!" Dawn suggested.

"That's a good one," Aunt Jane said.

"Getting dirty is not only acceptable, but encouraged!" Darby said.

"Fine with me," Aunt Jane said. "As long as your hands are clean when you eat."

"I know! I know!" I said, bouncing in my sneakers. I'd thought of a good one. "Everyone has to do a cartwheel at least once a day."

Aunt Jane shook her head. "Now, hang on, I'm not sure I can follow that one."

"Oh." I felt bad. Like I'd just spoiled a good game.

"I'm just not as spry as I used to be. But ..." Aunt Jane started making waving motions with her hands, as if trying to push all of us to one side. "Clear the way, you three. It's been several years since I've done a cartwheel, but let me try."

Dawn, Darby, and I moved off the grass and onto the cement square where the picnic table stood.

Aunt Jane stood with her arms straight down at her sides and stared hard at the stretch of grass in front of her. She opened and closed her hands a couple of times, took one step, and kind of rocked forward and back on her feet.

"You can do it, Aunt Jane!" I hollered.

With a whoosh, Aunt Jane raised her arms and whirled around in a cartwheel. It was great! Her legs were kind of bent and she made a noise like "*wah!*" but she did it! We all cheered, and then did cartwheels of our own.

"You know what we need?" Aunt Jane asked, as we reassembled at the picnic table. "A motto."

"Yeah!" my sisters and I said in unison.

"Like what?" I asked.

"Well, I just thought of one as you all did your cartwheels," Aunt Jane said. "How about 'United in Fun'?"

Dawn suggested we vote to make it official, and it was unanimous in favor.

"Good job, team. Let's finish up with the breakfast cleanup and then go down to the horse riding area," Aunt Jane said as she dried the cast-iron skillet. "You know, horse riding was always your mother's favorite part of our trips here."

"Aunt Jane, did you and Mom argue when you were camping? Or were you united in fun?"

"Well . . ." Aunt Jane ducked her head and looked a little

guilty again. "Let's just say I used to chase her with daddy longlegs. I'm not proud."

"Sounds kind of like Darby," Dawn said. "She loves picking up daddy longlegs."

Darby shook her head. "But I wouldn't chase anyone with them. That was kind of mean of you," she said to Aunt Jane.

"It sure was," Aunt Jane said. "Don't worry, your mom got revenge."

"What happened?"

"So later that same day, your mom and I were eating pinto beans with our smoked brisket, and I was trying to ruin her appetite by sticking beans in my nostrils."

"*Eww!*" exclaimed Dawn.

"That's mean, too!" Darby said, but she was giggling.

"What'd Mom do?" I asked.

"She . . . um . . . she tossed her milk in my face and I ended up inhaling beans. Dang near choked, too. But I tell you what — I never tried that again."

We laughed so hard, the birds in the nearby trees all flew away.

I love camping, and I love Aunt Jane. Camping plus Aunt Jane equals united in fun.

CHAPTER FOUR

Antagonize

Dawn

I knew Aunt Jane thought the horses would get us all excited, and it was nice of her to walk us out to the pasture. But while Darby and Delaney skipped along the gravel road, I lagged behind. I didn't want to say it out loud, but horses scare me. Darby is always going on about how smart they are and how much they helped shape society. Delaney thinks they are adorable and wants to have at least a couple as pets. Me? I think they look like wild giants who could stomp you to death.

It was bad enough that I already almost drowned. Now I was probably going to end up a bloody pulp for no good reason. It was hard to get enthusiastic about that.

"I hope they have a paint horse. That's what I want to ride," Delaney was saying. She was half running, half dancing down the lane and occasionally had to double back so that she didn't get too far away from us. All that motion was stirring up little tornadoes of dirt, and it would still be hanging in the air as I reached the same spot. The dust was sticking to my sweaty, sunblock-covered skin, making me look like a giant snickerdoodle.

But as fast as Delaney's feet were moving, her mouth, as usual, was moving even faster. "Someday I want my own paint horse. One with brown spots and a white mane. I think I want a mare, but a boy horse would be fine, too. And I could name it Dip Cone, because when I eat dip cones with the chocolate shell over vanilla, it makes me think of paint horses."

"That's a lousy name for a horse, Delaney," I said. "Nobody wants to be called a dip."

"Well . . . I also think of paint horses when I have black cows. The ice cream in the root beer makes the same kinds of patterns."

"Naming a horse Black Cow would be worse than naming it Dip Cone," I said. "No horse wants to be called a cow."

"Jiminy! She can name her horse whatever she wants to, Dawn," Darby said.

"She doesn't have a horse!"

Darby shook her head in a disappointed way. "You sure are grouchy, Dawn."

"I also think of paint horses when I eat chocolate sundaes," Delaney went on. "So I could name it Sundae — or maybe Sunday, with a *y*, like the day of the week."

She looked at me to see if I was going to say anything, but I didn't. I thought it was silly of her to name an animal she didn't have yet and never would because our mom won't let her. But Sundae was an improvement. Besides, I did sound like a big grouch, even though I didn't mean to. I was just sticky and grimy and not looking forward to getting kicked to death. Plus, my shoes still squished.

I checked to see if Aunt Jane was disappointed in me and my rants, but she was in front of me so I couldn't tell if she was frowning or not. I quickened my step to pull alongside her. When I looked over again, I noticed she was staring straight into the distance and seemed puzzled. Her brow was all scrunched and her head tilted to the left.

"What's wrong, Aunt Jane?" I asked.

"Huh? Oh . . . nothing. The place just seems different from the last time I was here."

"How so?"

"Well, for one thing, I don't see any people. Normally there are other campers headed to the rides, and camp workers helping out."

I strained my neck to look beyond the fence, and she was right. We were the only people around.

"Um . . . Aunt Jane? Where are the horses?" Darby asked.

We all glanced around, and sure enough, no horses were in sight. Just a few lazy cows walking and eating among the flies and mosquitos.

"There's the barn, right at the end of that drive," Aunt Jane said. She pointed to a red wood structure amid a few live oak trees at the end of a dirt lane.

"Maybe they just aren't out yet," Delaney said. "Can we go take a peek?"

Aunt Jane shrugged. "I don't see why not." But she hadn't even finished her sentence before Delaney took off like a shot followed closely by Darby, which sent another big cloud of dust over me.

"Hey!" I shouted, patting my arms to try and brush off the new layer of grime.

"I guess we better join them," Aunt Jane said to me. "Race you?"

"You go ahead. I'll be along in a bit," I said.

I didn't want to race — or run at all. I didn't even want to be there. But I managed to smile a little as I said it so that I didn't seem cranky.

Aunt Jane jogged off after them and I took my time catching up. On the way, I let out a lot of my grumbles about the bugs, the heat, my creek-water smell, and my grubby legs. But the thing I griped the most about was that boy, Jay, who'd said he wanted to be president. Like it was no big deal. Like he was saying he wanted tacos for dinner.

Some people have no respect for the office.

I hoped all my complaining would be done with by the time I reached the barn. But when I got there, everyone else looked as sullen as I felt. Darby was sitting on a hay bale, frowning down at her sneakers. Delaney was leaning over one of the stable gates, making it swing back and forth. The old metal hinges made a terrible screechy sound, as if they were wailing in protest. And Delaney was so crestfallen she looked like she might start wailing, too.

There were hoofprints in the dried mud of the stable floor, and some broken tack in the tack room, but there weren't any actual horses in sight.

Aunt Jane was talking in a cheery tone. "Maybe they're just out being ridden."

"I'm pretty sure that horses haven't been in here in a while," Delaney said.

"How can you be so sure?" Aunt Jane asked.

"This barn seems sorely neglected," Delaney said.

"Abandoned," Darby said.

"Practically ramshackle," I said.

"And besides, there's no . . . no . . ." Darby faltered.

"Because there's no manure," I finished for her. "Normally you can smell it from half a mile away."

Aunt Jane took a big sniff. "Huh. You're right," she said. "I wonder what happened. Last time I was here, horse riding was one of the most popular attractions."

"So we walked out here for nothing?" I asked. On one hand, I was relieved that I wouldn't get trampled, after all. But I could have spared myself the long, dusty trip out there.

"I just don't understand it," Aunt Jane kept saying, shaking her head. Her eyes darted around the room, but her gaze seemed faraway — as if she were painting over the sight of the old barn with memories of how it used to look.

As perturbed as I was, it made me sad to see her disappointed.

Darby ran over and threw her arms around Aunt Jane's middle. Aunt Jane blinked fast a few times, then she smiled.

"I don't mean to seem blue," she said, mussing up Darby's hair. "It's just that I always felt this place was special, and I really wanted to share it and have y'all love it, too."

"I know I'm going to love it," Delaney said. "I love everything you love."

"I love it already," Darby said.

Everyone looked at me. It made my cheeks feel tingly.

I really wanted to say that I love it or that I was sure I would love it. I even started the sentence. I said, "I . . ."

But then I started thinking about the stinky creek water and the lopsided camper and those lousy boys who didn't know anything about being a president but thought they did and the dust and lack of horses and . . .

I couldn't see myself, but I was pretty sure my grumpy face was coming back. And even though Darby and Delaney made big eyes at me, I never did finish the sentence. I couldn't lie.

"You know what?" Darby said. "I think this old barn is great. Let's explore, okay, Delaney?"

"Okay," Delaney said. "Maybe we can find clues. Or maybe some other animals have moved in, like raccoons. Or maybe plunderers and scalawags hid their loot here!"

As they ran all around making phony "oohs" and "ahs," I walked up to Aunt Jane and said, "I'm sorry I'm not more excited."

"No reason to be sorry, Dawnie." Aunt Jane patted my shoulder. "I have to admit that the campground seems a shabby version of its former self. But maybe it will grow on you. There have been many places in my past that I didn't realize I loved until later, after memories built up."

She grinned at me and I could tell she wasn't mad. Aunt Jane hardly ever gets steamed. I guess Darby's a lot like her in that way.

"So let's go make ourselves some good memories, okay?"

"Deal." I headed into the tack room where my sisters were romping around. I was determined to make the best of things. Aunt Jane deserved that.

I had to admit, it was fairly interesting poking around the tumbledown barn. Darby and I found a rusty horseshoe and an empty burlap sack and an old rope bridle half hidden in the mulch-y floor. Aunt Jane called it a hackamore bridle. There were other broken pieces of tack — bits of leather and metal hinges — but we couldn't tell exactly what they were. Meanwhile, Delaney tried to find evidence of animal life. She was pretty sure she found a mouse hole, but that's about it. After that she went back to swinging on the creaky stall doors.

"See, Aunt Jane? We can still have fun out here," Darby

said. "Watch this." She ran out into the training ring, climbed the wooden fence, and started balancing along the top like a tightrope walker. Her outstretched arms wavered slightly as she went.

A cold shiver went down my sweaty back. I recognized my uneasy feeling. I had it the day before when she was swinging from the rope over the creek. I didn't listen to my nerves then and ended up sorry. This time I'd heed the warning.

"Darby?" I hollered out to her. "Come back!"

In the distance, a cow chewing its cud looked up at us. It looked annoyed — and kind of menacing. I could just see it losing its temper, breathing steam out of its big nostrils, and charging toward us, breaking through the fence and maybe stomping on Darby. I wasn't sure if cows were strong or ornery enough, but it seemed like a dangerous possibility.

"Hey, Darby," I called out. "I really think you should get down."

"Why? This is fun."

"No, it's not."

This time I saw Delaney and Darby exchange glances — which made me extra irritable because I'd been trying to exchange one of those glances with Delaney.

"You're going to get hurt," I explained. "I've got an ominous feeling about that cow."

Darby looked down and gave me a comforting smile. "It's fine. You should come up here."

I glanced at the cow. I really didn't like the look in its eyes. It seemed to hate me. "No," I said. "I'm not falling for that line again."

"I'll try it!" Delaney shouted. And here I'd thought she was on my side. I figured after our emergency meeting she would be ready to help me stop Darby from putting us in danger.

Like a short, pigtailed Benedict Arnold, Delaney scrambled on top of the fence and started walking along it behind Darby. The cow watched the whole time, its nostrils twitching.

"Aunt Jane," I said, pulling on the sleeve of her T-shirt. It went against our code of ethics — which was signed in ink and in a special file at home — for us to try to get another sister in trouble, but I couldn't help it. I was anxious and worn-out and frustrated that no one was listening to me. "Make them get down. They're going to get hurt."

"You're sweet to worry, but you know better than I do that they are smart and steady and capable. And I'm right here if anything goes wrong."

"But . . . But . . ." It was betrayal all around. Something terrible was about to happen and no one was listening to me!

"Fine!" I marched toward the fence where my sisters stood. "Fall and break your tails! Get run over by a cow! See if I care!" I hollered, stamping my foot. "It's fine with me! Fine! Fine! Fine!"

Suddenly, a sharp pain shot up my leg. It felt like someone was stabbing me with a thousand needles. Like raindrops of hot lava. Or an explosion of evil.

Looking down, I saw something brown moving across my left sneaker. I shook my foot and the thing moved faster. It even seemed to spread out and get bigger. That's when I realized it wasn't just one thing — it was dozens.

My lower leg was covered in fire ants.

CHAPTER FIVE

Establishment

Darby

Delaney and I felt bad about laughing at Dawn. In our defense, we couldn't see the ants. All we knew was that she suddenly started hopping around and stamping and shaking her left leg. How were we to know she was being eaten alive? We thought she was dancing the Cotton-Eyed Joe.

Unfortunately, Delaney has a hard time stopping laughing once she gets going, so even after we discovered the ants and helped Dawn yank off her shoe and slap away the bugs that were still crawling on her, Delaney kept giggling.

"I'm sorry," she'd say, and then crack up all over again.

Dawn sure was mad. She hollered at us, the ants, and even the flowers. "What are you staring at?" she yelled at a cow.

I felt really bad for her, though. Fire ants hurt a lot. I've only had one or two stings at a time, but she had lots. Some people are allergic and have to go to the hospital if they get stung. Luckily we aren't, but it's still mighty painful.

Aunt Jane said we should take Dawn to Camp HQ — a combination office and general store that had a first aid station. The walk from the pasture to HQ wasn't as long as the walk back to our campground, but Dawn had to go super slow.

Camp HQ was a wide wooden building near the lake. Part of it was a store that, according to the signs on the windows, sold things like bait and kerosene, and the other part was like a huge covered porch. The first thing I noticed when we came inside was how good it smelled. That's because it also had a lunch counter. There was a lady in the back slicing potatoes, and there were a couple of campers sitting in the big patio area, eating and looking out over the water.

Delaney held open the door, and Aunt Jane and I shuffled inside with Dawn between us.

"Well, hey there, Tammy!" Aunt Jane called out to the lady.

"Jane! You're back!" The lady ran over and hugged the side of Aunt Jane that wasn't holding Dawn. "It's been years!"

Aunt Jane shook her head. "Too long. Girls, this is Mrs. Kimbro. Her family owns this campground."

"Hi," Delaney and I said together. Poor Dawn could only whimper.

"You got any first aid for fire ant stings?" Aunt Jane asked.

"Oh, you poor thing." Mrs. Kimbro went behind the counter again and ducked down. "I have some cortisone cream and antihistamine. Set the patient down and elevate that foot."

Aunt Jane and I helped Dawn stretch out on a wooden bench, and Delaney, who had been carrying Dawn's still-squishy shoe, placed it under her ankle in order to lift up the foot. Mrs. Kimbro came back with her hands full of supplies. She gave Aunt Jane a tube of cream and told her to rub it on all the bites. Then she set down a bottle of Benadryl, a bottle of water, and a cold pack.

Aunt Jane got right to work applying the cream. Dawn kept shaking her leg and sucking in her breath.

"Sure hope that stuff works," Dawn said. "It feels like my skin is giving off sparks." There was a quiver in her voice and the dust on her face had stripes on it from where the tears ran down her cheeks. I went over and grabbed her hand. Dawn tries to pretend she never cries, so I knew she was embarrassed as well as hurt and angry.

"So where'd you run into these rascals?" Mrs. Kimbro asked Aunt Jane.

"We came with her," Delaney said. "We're her nieces."

Mrs. Kimbro laughed a husky laugh. "I meant the fire ants."

"Over by the barn," Aunt Jane said, motioning her thumb in the direction we came. "The girls and I were hoping to go for a ride."

"But there were just cows," Delaney said.

"And ants," Dawn added.

"I'm afraid we don't offer horse rides anymore. The liability insurance got too expensive." Mrs. Kimbro shook her head and her smile turned sad. "People just don't seem to do outdoorsy things as much these days. And when they do come, plenty of them bring their TVs and gaming devices. I don't stop them, but I wonder — why even bother coming out here?"

"Darby and I love outdoorsy things," Delaney said to Mrs. Kimbro. "Don't we, Darby?"

I just nodded, feeling shy. Since this was my first time meeting Mrs. Kimbro, I avoided her eyes and looked past her at a metal sign on the wall that read UNATTENDED CHILDREN WILL BE GIVEN COFFEE AND A FREE BANJO.

"Darby here is like Tarzan," Delaney went on. "She can climb trees and jump high and isn't scared of anything."

I ducked my head. My cheeks felt like they'd been stung by something, too, even though it was a compliment.

"And I can run really fast, which is easier to do when you're outside," Delaney went on. "Plus, I love all animals. Even the poisonous ones and the ones who try to eat you. I just love them from far away."

"That's exactly why I brought you out here," Aunt Jane said. "People your age should spend lots of time outside. It's good for you. Fresh air. Exercise."

"Allergies. Mass insect attacks," Dawn muttered.

Aunt Jane finished putting the cream on Dawn's stings and patted her leg. "Aw, come on, Dawnie. What doesn't kill you makes you tougher."

"That doesn't make me feel better," Dawn snipped, crossing her arms over her chest.

Mrs. Kimbro really did have a wonderful laugh — scratchy but tuneful, like a mockingbird with a sore throat. "I see a real resemblance, Jane. These girls are definitely related to you and Annie."

I decided that I liked Mrs. Kimbro. She had golden hair that reminded me of hay in the sunshine, and she grinned all the time. But it wasn't always the same smile. It would be a small smile or a surprised smile or a gigantic happy one.

"Thanks for your help, Tammy," Aunt Jane said. "Sorry to interrupt your lunch prep."

"Nonsense. Anything for an old pal."

"That's a shame about the horse rides. Annie and I spent many happy hours out there." Aunt Jane stared out the window in the direction of the pasture.

Mrs. Kimbro let out a heavy sigh. "Times are tough. If it isn't finances and upkeep, it's this dang weather. We only have the old causeway for fishing now. The drought we had these past few years dried up most of the south end of the lake where the dock was."

"Still got the swimming beach with the canoes?"

"Sure do." Mrs. Kimbro nodded. "They aren't in the best of shape, but they're there. Though it's swim at your own risk."

"Not to worry," Aunt Jane said. "I'll keep an eye on the girls."

"Well, I better finish those wedge fries."

"Let me help. It's the least I can do."

Aunt Jane followed Mrs. Kimbro over to the grill and started washing her hands in the nearby sink. Soon I could hear them chuckling and talking about old times. I wonder if Mrs. Kimbro ever saw Aunt Jane chase Mom with daddy longlegs, or if she'd heard about the bean incident. It was funny to think that people knew things about my family that I didn't. I decided that I'd ask Mrs. Kimbro to tell me stories of Mom and Aunt Jane when they were younger, once the lunch rush was over.

"I want to go home," Dawn said as soon as Aunt Jane walked away. "This place hates me."

"No!" I exclaimed. "Not yet. We only just got here yesterday."

"Will you look at me?" Dawn gestured to her left leg, which was glossy from the cream. I could see the swelling and all the raised red dots from the ant stings. "If I stay here any longer, I'll end up struck by lightning."

"But we still haven't fished or boated or seen any wild animals or even explored all that much. And you're the only one who's gone swimming!" Delaney said.

"I did *not* go swimming. I fell into creek water that was full of slime!" Dawn's voice was becoming higher and squeakier. "I'm not like the two of you. You guys don't mind risking your life, but I do. I'm telling you, this place has it in for me."

"But fire ants are all over the place. What happened to you could have happened to any of us," I said.

"Not me. I always keep a look out for . . ." Delaney finally noticed my big warning eyes. "I mean . . . yeah. It was random."

I felt awful for Dawn. She'd already suffered two debacles — even though we'd only been there a day.

We always stick together. If one of us feels powerfully about something, the other two will usually back them up — after meetings where we debate, come to a decision, and hold a vote to make it legitimate. Only Dawn's reasons for leaving the campground weren't logical. She wasn't up to deliberating, though; she was downright woeful. If she needed to leave, we would leave. I knew she'd do the same for us.

"Okay," I said. "We'll talk to Aunt Jane."

Delaney gave me a pleading look. I raised my eyebrows and stared right back at her, silently reminding her of our one-for-all-and-all-for-one philosophy. After a couple of seconds, her shoulders sagged. "Fine. We'll ask Aunt Jane if we can go home."

"Thanks," Dawn said. She reached out and grabbed our hands. "You're probably saving my life."

Right at that moment, the screen door creaked open and in walked Jay, Robbie, and Nelson. They were wearing long shorts and wide-brimmed hats and hiking boots. Jay also had on a big backpack.

As soon as she saw them, Dawn turned away and her

cheeks darkened to the color of a Coke can. She grabbed a napkin out of a nearby dispenser and began dabbing at her face, real slowly, so that from behind it wouldn't be too obvious what she was doing.

"Hi there!" Delaney called out. She didn't seem to notice that Dawn was all hunkered over in shame.

"Hi," Robbie called back.

Nelson leaned toward Jay and whispered, "It's those girls who were spying on us." Jay nodded.

"What's up?" Jay asked us.

"Dawn got attacked by a million fire ants," Delaney said, gesturing toward Dawn's outstretched leg. "Now she wants us to quit camping and go home."

Poor Dawn looked like she wanted a lightning bolt to hit her right then. "No, I don't!" she said. "I was just kidding when I said that."

Delaney looked baffled. She knew Dawn was lying. I knew it, too, but it didn't matter. I turned around so that Delaney could see me but the boys couldn't and made my eyes extra wide as a signal. "Yeah, Delaney," I said. "Even I knew Dawn was joking. Don't tell me you believed her."

When you're a triplet, sometimes you let yourself look foolish so that one of your sisters can preserve her dignity. And sometimes, if one sister is feeling particularly miserable, you make the other sister look like a fool. It may not seem fair, but it kind of is. Because one day you'll be the miserable one.

Again, it took Delaney a while to notice my big buggy eyes.

"Oh. Right. Ha-ha-ha. I should have known it was a joke. You . . . joker." Delaney gave Dawn's shoulder a soft bump with her fist.

I didn't like contradicting Delaney like that in front of those guys, and I knew she was embarrassed. That's called "losing face." But I figured she could take it. Dawn had already lost a lot of face. Any more and she'd be just a head of hair.

"So what are you guys up to?" I asked Jay, Robbie, and Nelson. Normally I'm not this chatty with strangers, but I felt a big urge to change the subject.

"We're going on an expedition and need supplies," Nelson said.

"An expedition? That sounds like fun!" Delaney started bouncing on her toes. "Can we come?"

I had the very same words in my head, only I didn't say them aloud.

The boys looked at one another. "Um . . . Sorry, but I don't think so. It's already planned out," Jay said. "You see, we have ways of doing things. It's sort of like . . . a mini government. You wouldn't understand."

Dawn, Delaney, and I exchanged surprised glances. Well, Dawn's glance was more of a glower.

At that point, all six of us were just standing there, but no one was saying anything. After a while the silence felt weird.

"Okay, well . . . see ya," Jay said. He pivoted around on his hiking boots and headed for the snack display with Nelson right behind him.

Robbie smiled at us and gave a small wave. Then he trotted fast to catch up with the other boys.

Delaney and I waved back, but Dawn just scowled. Dawn had been surly ever since we first discovered those boy campers. I'm not sure why she saw them as a threat. I didn't exactly like them, but I didn't dislike them, either.

"So . . . now that we said we're staying at the campground, does this mean we're actually staying?" Delaney asked.

"Of course," Dawn said, still frowning at the boys' backs. "No way am I giving those fellows the satisfaction of us leaving."

Delaney shouted, "Yay!" and I high-fived her. I went to give Dawn a high five, but she had her arms folded across her chest.

"But I have another ominous feeling," Dawn said, "that this campground isn't big enough for the six of us."

CHAPTER SIX

Association

Delaney

We decided to have lunch at Camp HQ instead of our campsite so that Dawn could stay off her feet a while longer and let the medicine work. The skin on her leg was all pink and the stings had blistered. It reminded me of chicken skin. So when Aunt Jane suggested the chicken tenders, I said "No, thank you" and asked for grilled cheese instead. It was yummy, but then I gobbled it lickety-split and ended up with nothing to do.

I don't understand how Mom and Lily say "time flies," because to me it's the opposite. To me, time moves like a sleepy snail or molasses running uphill. My sisters didn't seem bored. Across the table from me, Dawn was staring off into the distance, tapping her chin, and occasionally grumbling to herself. She was probably pondering something related to those boys. Darby sat beside me, lost in la-la land, slowly eating the rest of her crinkle chips. Darby is the most adventuresome of the three of us, but she's also the day-dreamiest. She can sit still for hours just thinking or doodling or reading. Then again, the way she was tilted toward the long wooden counter made me wonder if she were trying to eavesdrop on Aunt Jane and Mrs. Kimbro, who stood talking on the other side.

I drummed my fingers on the table, but the rhythm just made me want to dance around more. I bounced on the wooden bench a bit, but that wasn't any fun since it had no cushion.

"I feel antsy," I said to Dawn.

She grimaced. "Please don't use that word around me."

"Oh. Sorry."

I glanced around searching for a distraction. Over by the cash register was a tall circular rack full of postcards. There were lots with wildflowers on the front, and some with wild animals. My favorite was of a bobcat with big round yellow eyes.

"Aunt Jane, can I buy a postcard?" I asked.

"Good idea. As long as we're here, why don't you girls all pick out postcards and write messages to folks back home?" She turned to Mrs. Kimbro. "Got any stamps?"

"Yes, ma'am." Mrs. Kimbro headed over to the cash register, opened it, and pulled out three stamps. "Here, darling," she said, setting them on the table by Dawn.

"Thanks," we all said.

Mrs. Kimbro's grin widened. "Sure thing. I've also got a cup full of pens and pencils up here. Y'all help yourself to whatever you need. When you're done you can post them there." She pointed to the door near the patio. Next to it stood a tall wooden box with the words OUTGOING MAIL stenciled on it in dark blue.

It took a few minutes for me to look over all the options. Finally, I decided to get two with the bobcat picture. It was still my favorite.

"You guys want any?" I asked Dawn and Darby.

Darby shook her head. "Postcards are too small — I can't fit a proper letter on them."

"Dawn, do you want one?" I asked.

"Maybe. Are there any with pictures of fire ants on them? I want everyone back home to see the danger they've put us in."

I looked and looked, but there were no ant postcards.

"Fine," Dawn said when I told her. "Is there one of anything that crawls on the ground?"

"There's a horned toad."

"Perfect."

I also grabbed pens for both me and Dawn and sat down beside her. I wrote *Dear Mom,* on one card and *Dear Dad,* on the other. Then I couldn't think of anything else to write. That pins-and-needles feeling was back. It wasn't that I was bored exactly. It was that I could feel all the places outside that I hadn't explored — all the things I hadn't seen yet. I just didn't want to sit any longer.

But then I remembered one of our rules for home and campground: *No going off by yourself.*

I glanced over at Darby, who had secured some notebook paper from Mrs. Kimbro and was in the process of composing a letter — filling the lines with her itty-bitty scrawl. In front of her was a stack of empty sheets and a few envelopes. No way could I wait for her to finish writing.

I looked over at my other sister, who seemed almost done with her postcard.

"So, Dawn," I began in my friendliest voice. "It seems like you're feeling better. Would you like to go for a walk when you're done with that card?"

"You got the pent-up jitters, don't you?" she asked without glancing up.

I hung my head a little. "Yes. I can't help it. I want to go search for real bobcats, not just gaze at their pictures."

"Ding-dang it, Delaney. Do you want to get scratched to pieces? Considering my mishaps, Darby's daredevil antics, and you wanting to befriend wild animals, Aunt Jane is going to end up taking us all to the hospital!"

"Don't worry, I wouldn't get too close." The restless feelings were making me bounce on my toes. "I just want to see *something.*"

I wanted to say that I was jealous of Jay, Robbie, and Nelson because they got to go on an expedition. They'd probably already seen bobcats or jack rabbits or baby deer. But I knew those guys were a sore spot with Dawn, so I pressed my lips together hard to keep the words from escaping.

Dawn let out a big loud sigh. "Just go. Turn more cart-wheels or something. Unlike me, you've got two good feet, so you should use them. As long as you stay close, Aunt Jane won't worry."

"You're right! That's still a lot of space," I said, taking tiny hops closer to where Aunt Jane and Mrs. Kimbro were laughing over something. "Aunt Jane, I'm going outside, but will stay in sight of HQ, okay?"

"Sure thing, Delaney," she said, turning to look at the three of us. "Why don't you take your apple in case you want a quick bite?" I nodded and went back to get it.

"Here," Dawn handed me her postcard. "Can you put this in the mail drop on the way out?"

I didn't mean to read her private message, but Dawn has big writing and the mail drop was on the far end of HQ. This is what it said:

Dear Mom,

Wish you were here. Actually more than that, I wish I wasn't here. But since I am and you aren't, I wish you were here to see how boring and treacherous it is. Then maybe you'll think twice about ever sending us camping.

Love,
Dawn

P.S. Please tell Dad. I'm too traumatized to write this all over again.

After I plunked it in the mail slot, I skipped outside and started turning cartwheels on the grassy area by the patio in order to get the jitters out. Then I headed toward the trees, careful not to get out of sight of Camp HQ, so that Aunt Jane could still see me if she checked.

I slipped off my sandals to be extra quiet, and scanned the nearby wilderness, searching for the tufted ears of a bobcat, but all I could see were leaves and branches and rocks. I also looked for horned toads, but didn't spot any. There were lots and lots of orange and yellow wildflowers, though. That was pretty.

Scouring for animals was not as fun as I thought it would be. Eventually, my eyes got tired and my body got fidgety again, so I started tossing my apple up and catching it. Then I tried catching it one-handed and only missed a couple of times. Once it was on the ground, I started to kick it back and forth like a soccer ball. This was fun for a while, until I stepped on a prickle burr and it got stuck in the heel of my foot.

As I sat down on the grass to pull it out, I heard a rustling in the bushes near me. Looking closer, I spotted fur-covered ears! At first I thought it might be a bobcat, but they weren't the right shape. Instead, they looked a lot like jack rabbit ears. But I knew that couldn't be right, either — because they were way too high off the ground. Unless it was a giant mutant jack rabbit?

The ears twitched and started moving toward me. Whatever it was, it sounded big. Because its footsteps made heavy *tamp-tamp*ing sounds. I figured I should run away and give it space, but the burr was still stuck in my foot. And then suddenly, the thing in the bushes made a horrible, blaring noise like a broken tuba.

I couldn't help it. I let out one of my intolerably loud screams and started crawling backward. I was about to get eaten!

Out of the corner of my eye I saw Aunt Jane, Mrs. Kimbro, and Darby dash out the door of HQ and race toward me. But they were far away, and at the very same moment the beast pushed its way through the brush.

I saw those twitchy, rabbit-like ears, and below that, a long muzzle. At the end of the muzzle was a mouth that opened wide, revealing huge yellow-and-brown teeth. Before I could scream again, the mouth came down down down . . .

. . . and started chomping on my apple.

Dear Mom,

I made a friend at camp. It's a donkey! We named him Mo. He's really smart and has the cutest ears. I know you said I couldn't have a horse, but how about a donkey? Please think about it. Please please please. I promise to wake up early every morning to feed and brush him and will even shovel up his messes. Mrs. Kimbro says donkey manure is good fertilizer, so I could put it on the rose bushes.

Love,
Delaney

CHAPTER SEVEN

Cooling-Off Period

Dawn

When we heard Delaney's scream, we all shot out of HQ like rockets — well, I moved more like a hurried zombie with my itchy leg and only one shoe on.

By the time I made it out there, she'd gotten over her fright and was laughing and patting that ugly donkey on his forehead. She would be mad if she knew I referred to him that way, but it's the truth. He's about the funniest looking animal I've ever seen.

Delaney and Darby started fawning all over the beast as if he were a big puppy. And there I was, trying to balance on one squishy sneaker. To tear everyone away, Aunt Jane reminded us that we were due our Daily Chocolate according to our camping guidelines. This made Darby and Delaney agree to go back to HQ, with me hobbling after them.

Mrs. Kimbro told us all about the donkey as we shared a small package of Oreos. The donkey belongs to her family and is allowed to wander free most of the time because he's very gentle. Mrs. Kimbro said he's getting kind of old and that his real name is Donkey — which is a lousy name, even if it is technically accurate. Apparently, Darby didn't like it, either, because she suggested nicknaming him Democrat, or Mo for short. We all agreed that this fit him better and decided to call him Mo while we were there.

Then Mrs. Kimbro told us how Donkey/Mo had been good friends with their dog, a shepherd mix named Chiquita. But she died last winter and Mo has been lonely ever since.

"Poor thing!" Darby exclaimed.

"I'll be his new friend!" Delaney said, and I could see her eyes starting to tear up over the story.

I have to admit, I also felt sorry for the poor animal.

When we left HQ and headed back to our camper, Mo followed us the entire way. Darby and Delaney were overjoyed. As friendly as he was, I still kept a safe distance. Donkeys are smaller than horses and cows, and Mrs. Kimbro said he was no trouble. Still, I'm pretty sure he could flatten me with his hooves if he wanted to — so I wasn't going to give him a reason to want to.

Back at camp, Darby went into the trailer to finish her letter home. Mo started eating some plants over by our cartwheel spot, and Delaney proceeded to follow him around, telling him her life story.

I decided to spend more time with Aunt Jane. She was sitting at the picnic table staring out at the nearby trees with that same faraway expression she'd been wearing a lot lately.

"It must be so boring for you here," I said, sitting down beside her.

Aunt Jane looked surprised. "Not at all. I love camping. Remember, it was my idea to bring you all out here."

"I mean coming back to rural Texas. Boston must be so much better."

"Oh, honey, no. It's not better."

"But it's big and old and it has all those museums. Revolutionary War heroes actually lived and worked there!" I rested my chin on my hand and let out a sigh of longing. "It must be so much more exciting."

"My last two days there were spent going to work, ordering supplies, making phone calls, coming home, and sleeping. My two days here have involved you falling into a creek and getting attacked by ants, cartwheels, running into a dear old friend, and Delaney getting freaked out by a donkey. I ask you" — she bumped my shoulder with hers — "which sounds more exciting?"

"You know what I mean. Boston has all that history. It has everything."

"It's just different, that's all. The weather is different. The traffic is different. There aren't as many donkeys walking around. But in most ways, it's not so different. There are good folks there and folks you want to avoid. And remember, history is everywhere — not just in museums."

"I guess."

"Besides there's one huge thing Boston doesn't have." Aunt Jane smiled slyly.

"What's that?"

"My family," she said, pointing right at me. "Don't forget about family history. It's precious, and we're making it right now. Together."

I thought about that for a second. Aunt Jane always made us feel remarkable. When other kids teased us and refused to play Presidential Trivia or do re-enactments of important historical moments, she told us it didn't make us weird — it made us exceptional. That was the word she used, and I loved it. We were an exception.

"Thanks, Aunt Jane!" I reached over and gave her a big hug. Once again she looked surprised.

"Aw, shucks," she said, patting out a rhythm on my back. "If I've helped you in some way, then it's my pleasure."

I used to wonder what it was like for the president of the United States to live and work in the same house. Surely it would be distracting, and sometimes annoying, to have family so close by. But just now, I realized it was a bonus.

Because sometimes it's your family that teaches you things the way no one else can. Not experts or philosophers or elder statesmen — but family.

"Aunt Jane, when I become president, would you be one of my top advisors?"

"It would be a great honor, Dawnie."

Dear Lily,

How are you? How's Alex? Camping has been ~~fun~~ ~~great~~ interesting.

I love the flowers here, and the animals. Especially all the birds — I've seen finches and jays and doves and warblers. I think when they look down at Lake Lewis, they probably don't see that it's broken into campsites and neutral zones. They probably just see trees and grass and lakes. Perhaps in their minds, there are only two different places — their nest and everywhere else.

I think I would like to be a bird. Birds are maybe the only creatures that see the world the right way.

But since I can't be one, I'll settle for a window seat in an airplane the next time we go on vacation — hopefully with you there, too.

Love you,
Darby

CHAPTER EIGHT

Operation Cheer Up Aunt Jane

Darby

When I woke up the next morning, Aunt Jane was asleep on her bunk, but Dawn and Delaney weren't there. Peering out the window flap, I could see Delaney feeding Mo some of our carrots.

By the time I got outside, Mo was done with the carrots and Delaney was waving different kinds of leaves and grasses in front of his face.

"Where's Dawn?" I asked, glancing around.

Delaney pointed toward the other side of the campground. "She went to see if the boys were holding a meeting so she could listen in."

I shook my head. Once Dawn sets her mind on something, she's like our golden Labrador, Quincy, when he picks up the scent of a cat. She stays focused on it no matter what, and has been known to howl if she's kept from her goal.

"I need to go to HQ and mail my letter to Lily," I said, holding up the sealed envelope. "Plus, I need to buy more stamps for all the other letters I'm going to write. Would you come with me so that I'll be following the rules?"

"Sure! Come on, Mo."

I crept back into the camper and silently wrote out a note for Aunt Jane. Then we headed toward HQ. As we passed him, Mo fell into step behind us. I hated to think how Delaney was going to react when it was time to leave the campground, and Mo, behind.

Just as we reached the opening in the brush that led to the trail, we heard Dawn's voice behind us.

"Hold up!" She ran over and wedged in between me and Delaney. "Where are you headed? Can I come?"

"To HQ and sure," I said. "What have you been doing?"

"Those boys were holding a morning meeting and I . . ." She paused. "I just happened to overhear them."

"Are you still bothered by Jay wanting to be president?" Delaney asked.

"Please," she said, waving her hand as if flicking away the question. "I pity the guy, actually. If I wasn't so busy, I'd go over there and give him pointers."

"What's he doing wrong?" I asked.

"He's letting each boy lobby for how he thinks they should spend the day. The speeches are taking forever! I finally got bored and snuck away."

I was going to ask her why she was spying on them if she doesn't care what they do, but decided it was best to let the conversation end. Besides, we were coming up on HQ.

An older man with a bushy gray mustache was heading the opposite way down the other trail that led to the lake. He was carrying a fishing pole and had a big green satchel hanging off his right shoulder. "Good morning, good morning, good morning," he said, tipping his fishing cap at each of us as we filed past.

"Good morning," we said.

Then he tipped his hat at Mo. "Good morning, Mr. Donkey."

Mo made a snuffly sound.

"Name's Ned Bartholomew," he said. "To whom do I have the pleasure of introducing myself?"

"We're Dawn, Darby, and Delaney Brewster," Delaney said, pointing at each of us when she said our names.

"Honored to make your acquaintance," Mr. Bartholomew said. I couldn't see his mouth because of his big moustache, but I could tell by his eyes that he was smiling. "Y'all have a terrific day now." He gave us a teeny bow and continued on his way.

"You too," we called out.

"He's nice," I said once he'd walked out of range.

"He is," Delaney said. "He kind of reminds me of Mr. Neighbor, only he doesn't say 'Make way for ducklings!'"

"He could have said, 'Make way for donkeys!'" Dawn said, and we all laughed.

Camp HQ was the busiest we've seen it since we arrived. There were about five other people inside, all wearing floppy hats and carrying fishing poles or thermoses. Mrs. Kimbro was running all around, working the cash register, finding special tackle, and serving up the daily breakfast special — pigs in blankets. I plopped my letter into the OUTGOING MAIL box and we got in line at the counter.

When Mrs. Kimbro spotted us she waved and wished us a good morning. "How can I help you?"

Even though she's probably one of the nicest people I'd ever met, I was still feeling shy and hesitated before replying. Just as I was opening my mouth to answer, Delaney jumped in. "She needs more stamps for all the letters she's going to write," she said, pointing at me.

"Here you go, darling. I'll put it on Jane's tab." Mrs. Kimbro placed a book of stamps on the counter, and I managed to look her in the eye, smile, and say thanks. "So what adventures do you three girls have planned for today?"

"Nothing yet," Dawn said.

"Also, we don't usually plan our adventures," Delaney said. "They just seem to find us."

"I see. Is Jane with you?" she asked, glancing around.

Dawn shook her head. "Nope. Aunt Jane runs a tavern, so she is used to staying up late and not getting up really early."

"That's right. She did tell me that. She said it was good to be out here seeing lots of daylight for a change. Poor thing." Mrs. Kimbro made one of her semi-sad smiles. "Now if y'all will excuse me, I'm still shorthanded and need to finish some tasks."

Mrs. Kimbro's words jostled a thought in my brain. Something that I'd ponder anytime I wasn't busy. As soon as we stepped back outside where Mo was waiting, I glanced around to make sure no one was listening and then put a hand on each of my sisters.

"Y'all, listen. I'm worried about Aunt Jane," I said. "You know how you notice things when you watch people?"

"You mean like spying?" Dawn asked.

I hunched my shoulders. "Not exactly. I mean the way people look when they don't know you're looking at them."

"So . . . a little bit like spying?" Delaney asked.

I let out a sigh. "What I mean is I've been observing Aunt Jane when she thinks no one sees her, and she doesn't seem very happy."

"She has looked rather glum," Delaney said.

Dawn nodded. "Forlorn."

"And I think it's pretty clear what's wrong," I said.

"What?" Delaney asked.

"It's because she sees how different the campground is, how rundown it's getting, and it makes her sad."

Dawn shook her head. "I think it makes her bored. What we're seeing is homesickness. She could be doing more exiting and important stuff in Boston. She's used to a big city, and a half-empty campground just can't compete."

"You're both wrong," Delaney said. "Aunt Jane is worn-out from taking care of us. Think about it — she has to spend her vacation from work babysitting us instead of relaxing. We need to show her that we're old enough and responsible enough to take care of ourselves. Then she can have some fun. And maybe she'll tell Mom when we get back that we can take care of ourselves."

"I'm all for that," I said, "but how are we going to convince Aunt Jane that we're mature and reliable?"

We stood there, silently contemplating. I looked at Dawn, Dawn looked at Delaney, and Delaney looked at Mo, who started snuffling around the ground for something to eat.

Suddenly, Delaney started hopping up and down. "I know! I know! I know!" She lifted her chin triumphantly and said, "We'll make her breakfast today!"

CHAPTER NINE

Melting Pot

Delaney

We wanted breakfast to be a surprise, and maybe even serve it to Aunt Jane in her bunk — but she was already sitting at the picnic table when the three of us (four, if you count Mo) got back to the campsite. Her hair was sticking out in all directions again, like a brown sea anemone sitting on her head.

"Good morning, girls!" she greeted us, lifting her cup of instant coffee. "What do you want for breakfast?"

"To make it," I replied.

Aunt Jane's eyebrows went up so high they disappeared under the soft tentacles of her curls.

"It's true," Dawn said. "We've decided to take care of the meal, so don't worry about a thing."

Aunt Jane looked like she might be worried about a thing. Maybe two. "What brought this on?" she asked.

"We're just being nice," Darby said.

"And responsible," Dawn said.

"And older," I said.

"Well, all right, then," Aunt Jane said with a shrug. "Can I help?"

"Nope," we all said.

"What should I do while you three make breakfast?"

"Go back to sleep?" Darby suggested.

Aunt Jane shook her head. "Nope, I'm already wide-awake."

"I would say go watch cartoons. That's what I do when I'm waiting for breakfast back home. Only we don't have a TV. So maybe . . ." I tried to think of a grown-up task — things Mom and Dad usually tell us they need to do. "Check the van's tire pressure?"

Dawn rolled her eyes at me. "You can do whatever you like," she said to Aunt Jane. "The point is that we'll take care of everything."

Aunt Jane grinned. "Well, that's mighty thoughtful of you girls. I guess I do have some tavern business to tend to. But y'all come fetch me if you need me. Deal?"

After she went back into the trailer, we held a brief meeting to decide what we should make. Darby suggested cereal, but Dawn said that wasn't impressive enough to show how responsible we are. Dawn suggested pancakes, but I reminded her of the Mother's Day Pancake-Making Fiasco of two years ago. (Mom still points to stains on the ceiling in our kitchen back home and grumbles about it.) Pancakes look light and fluffy and easy, but they can make huge messes. So I suggested another round of Spam and eggs, and, after tapping her chin a few times, Dawn declared that it was high protein and healthy, but not too difficult. Darby agreed.

I was so excited that my idea won, especially since I already knew how to make it.

Only we couldn't find any Spam. I poked my head into the trailer to ask Aunt Jane, and she told me she'd just bought one container — the one we used the day before.

So then we were back to square one. Dawn resumed pacing about, and Darby sat down at the picnic table and rested her chin on her hand. Meanwhile, I looked through the big cardboard box we were using as a food pantry and spied a couple of cans of beans. That gave me a new idea.

"I know!" I cried out. "Let's make a bean-and-egg scramble!"

Bean-and-egg scramble is what Dad likes to make for breakfast when he has time to cook. I didn't know the recipe, but I figured it couldn't be hard. It's basically scrambled eggs with beans in them. Dad likes to use black beans and top it with lots of grated cheese. It's pretty yum.

Dawn and Darby agreed that this would be an acceptable substitute for Spam and eggs. That meant I got two ideas approved! I was so thrilled, I did a little skippity-hoppity dance step. It reminded me a bit of Mynah and how we bounce around together in the mornings back home. I sure missed that rabbit, and I started wondering if maybe donkeys liked to bounce.

My thoughts were interrupted by Dawn waving her hand in front of my face and saying that if we wanted to help Aunt Jane and show we're responsible, we should make breakfast before lunchtime. Then she stood on the picnic table bench and started hollering out orders. She announced that I would be in charge of the eggs, Darby would be in charge of the beans, and she would set the table and pour the juice.

None of those tasks seemed very difficult, but for some reason everything went wrong.

First off, cracking eggs is hard. Well . . . the cracking part isn't. But the part where you open them up and get the eggs out is tricky. I kept getting bits of shell in the bowl along with the eggs. I tried to dig them out, but gave up after a while. "Eggs are going to be a tiny little bit crunchy," I said as I added them to the pan.

Once the eggs were almost cooked, I told Darby I was ready and she dumped the can of beans into the pan. Only it wasn't beans. The next thing I knew, lots of small fish in a red sauce was oozing over the eggs. It was the canned sardines Aunt Jane likes to snack on. The fishy smell hit us at the same time and Darby and I looked at each other in horror.

"Should I set out salt and pepper?" Dawn called out from the table, unaware of our big mistake.

"Uh . . . I don't think we're going to need it," I said.

I tried to sound matter-of-fact, but Dawn immediately guessed something was wrong and ran over to peer into the skillet.

She gasped. "What on earth is that?"

"Breakfast?" I said with a smile.

The look she gave me. *Sheesh!* You'd think I rigged an election or something.

We explained to her what happened, and I thought Darby was going to apologize for four score and seven years. But right at that moment, Aunt Jane came out of the trailer and took a big sniff. "Something is smelling loud," she said. "Is it time to eat yet?"

None of us said anything. We just stood there feeling sorrowful. Then Aunt Jane walked up, grabbed a plate, and scooped up a sizeable portion.

"*Mm-mm.* Hearty," Aunt Jane exclaimed after she took a bite. I couldn't believe she was eating it.

I guess that's love — eating whatever your family cooks, even if it's not a real recipe and tastes like cat food.

The three of us weren't sure what else to do, so we each ladled out a share and started eating — or trying to. Darby ate up hers, but then Darby will eat everything — except raisins or marshmallows. Dawn seemed to finish it, too. Of course, her serving was about the size of a donut hole.

I tried to eat my helping. I really did. But after a few bites it was like my stomach shut itself up, put on a padlock, and hung an OUT OF BUSINESS sign. I just couldn't get down another morsel. I pretended to accidentally leave my bowl out where Mo could get to it, but even he wouldn't eat it. After a few snorts he turned and tramped off to the other end of the campsite. I felt bad that our cooking scared him away.

"Sorry that the breakfast was kinda lousy," I said to Aunt Jane as we started clean-up.

"Yeah. Darby didn't mean to bungle everything," Dawn said.

"Your fish had a red label, just like the beans. I should have read it more carefully," Darby said in a sorrowful voice.

"Hey now." Aunt Jane's eyes went worried looking. "What's all this apologizing?"

The three of us hung our heads.

"We wanted to cheer you up and demonstrate our independence," I mumbled.

Aunt Jane stood up from the table and clapped her hands together twice. "All right, triplets. Huddle up!" she said, holding her arms outstretched.

I stepped into her left arm, Dawn stepped into her right and Darby stepped in between us. Then we all stepped forward and pressed our heads together.

"The point of breakfast is to nourish our bodies, and the point of doing something nice for someone is to show them you care," Aunt Jane said. "Therefore, the mission was accomplished."

"So . . . are you feeling happy?" I asked.

"I am!" she said, and we all shouted hurrah. "Today is going to be a great day. I just know it."

"You were going to take us swimming and boating today, right?" Darby asked.

"And we still have to do our Morning Cartwheels!" I reminded them.

"Yes to both of those things," Aunt Jane said, and we cheered again. "But . . . not just yet, okay?" She put her hands on her belly. "I'm going to need a little time to digest first."

CHAPTER TEN

American Dream

Dawn

It took about an hour to recover from breakfast. Eventually, Aunt Jane said it was time to go to swimming and boating. We did our Morning Cartwheels, changed into our swimsuits, applied sunscreen, and packed up a bag with towels, bottled water, and some granola bars and fruit.

Delaney tried to pretend that she wanted five apples as a snack, but Aunt Jane didn't fall for it.

"Mo is not our donkey, so we shouldn't feed him anything unless Mrs. Kimbro says it's all right. It might make him sick, and you wouldn't want that, would you?"

Delaney bowed her head. "No," she said in a teeny-tiny voice.

It didn't last, though. Soon she was skipping out of the camper ahead of me, Darby, and Aunt Jane, chattering about swimming. Delaney has fast feet and an even faster mouth, but she can shake off a bad mood quickly, too.

We followed Aunt Jane down a winding path toward the lake. Mo was with us most of the way, but once we got to the beach, we realized he was gone.

"He'll be back," Delaney said. "He loves being with us, but he's probably not much of a swimmer."

The swimming area was at a bend in the lake that had a long stretch of pebbled beach. The water was still and peaceful — and a lot cleaner looking than that mossy feeder creek I'd fallen into on the day we arrived.

"Wow. This place sure looks different than the last time I was here," Aunt Jane said.

"How?" Delaney asked.

"Well . . . the beach is bigger."

You could tell the lake level was down because of the old watermarks on the rock ledge across the cove and the dilapidated dock to our left. On our right, three scratched-up looking gray canoes sat on the beach. As soon they'd set down their stuff and kicked off their shoes, Darby and Delaney went to investigate.

"That's not a good sign," I said.

"What isn't?" Aunt Jane looked all around us.

"That sign," I said, pointing. Stuck in the gravel was a wooden plank with the following words painted on it:

NO LIFEGUARD ON DUTY
Swim at your own RISK

She grinned. "You'll be fine."

"I likely will be. But the sign says swim at your *own risk*. Darby's definition of risk is very different from mine or yours or any normal person. You know her. There could be gators in there and she'd probably still jump in."

Aunt Jane hunkered down so that her head was right next to mine. "It's all right," she whispered. "I'll keep an eye on all of you, especially Darby. I just want you to have fun."

Hopefulness was all over her face. I knew Aunt Jane wanted us to enjoy ourselves here, just like she and Mom did when they were little. But I also I knew that she was bored being away from Boston. If spending a few hours at a dangerous beach was her idea of a good time, I wouldn't stand in the way.

"I will," I assured her.

"Guys, come here!" Delaney hollered from down the beach. By the time Aunt Jane and I caught up with them, she was already trying to shove one of the canoes into the water. "Come on and help. There's enough seats here for all of us to go!"

I bent over to scratch my ant-bitten ankle, but otherwise stayed put. My nervousness was growing stronger — like turning up the volume on the car radio. I couldn't help noticing that the water looked murky and the boats looked rickety. I could see myself taking another deep plunge again, this time getting nibbled by snapping turtles.

I couldn't shake these feelings of impending doom, but I was also tired of being a big baby and I didn't want to ruin Aunt Jane's visit here.

"You guys go ahead," I said, trying to sound casual. "I just want to relax."

Before Delaney could do that bouncy pleading thing she always does, I turned and headed back to the swimming section. Soon I could hear fast footsteps behind me. I knew who it was before I saw her.

"Dawn, are you okay?" Darby asked. "Do you want us to tell Aunt Jane we want to go back to Mom's house?"

"No!" I hollered. I knew Darby was just trying to help, but I wanted to feel crabby instead of sorry for myself. At least when I'm mad, I feel powerful.

"Okay. It's just . . . you seem all woebegone. Yesterday you wanted to leave, but then changed your mind when you saw Jay, Robbie, and Nelson."

Thinking about those know-it-all boys increased the energizing, angry feelings. "So?" I said.

"So maybe we should just go home."

"No way! Aunt Jane loves it out here and she's stuck baby-sitting us, so no way are we ruining her fun. Besides, you're overreacting. All I said was that I was going to lie down on the beach for a while. Just because I don't want to go on a broken-down boat doesn't mean I'm ready to pack up my stuff."

Darby waited before saying anything. She had that

watchful, oh-so-patient look on her face that people use when talking with lunatics or toddlers. "So . . . you really do want to stay?" she asked finally.

"Of course," I said, with another nod.

"This isn't just you being prideful?"

"No," I said. There might have been a slight hesitation in my response.

Darby looked like she wanted to point at me and shout "Aha!" but she didn't, because she's Darby. Instead, she said, "Okay. But if you change your mind, let me know." Then she jogged back down to the canoes.

I knew she thought I was being bullheaded. And *she* knew that I knew that — but she still wasn't going to challenge me on it. Sometimes having an understanding sister can be annoying.

I spread my towel out on the smoothest, least pebbly stretch of ground I could find and lay down on it. I felt tired and hot. The sun was behind the tops of the trees, so my spot was shady, and every now and then a breeze would whoosh over me, cooling any sweaty parts. That's what made me think the hot was coming from inside me as much as from outside me.

I was just so mixed up. Perhaps I hadn't been thinking straight the day before when I said I wanted to go home. That was probably my embarrassment and frustration talking. Or maybe that was me being sensible? Maybe I hadn't been thinking straight when I swore to the boys yesterday, and to

Darby just now, that I wanted to stay at the campground. That was probably pride and pigheadedness talking.

All that contemplating was making me feel worn-out and drowsy — or it could have been the antihistamines Aunt Jane made me swallow for my ant bites. I closed my eyes and tried to broker peace between my battling thoughts. They didn't stop fighting, but they did get farther and farther away. Even the ground beneath me seemed to dissolve, and all around me sounds grew fainter . . .

I could see Delaney in front of me. She was trying to teach Mo how to juggle apples while Darby did handstands on his back. I kept yelling at them to be careful but they couldn't hear me. I tried to get closer to them, but couldn't move for some reason. Looking down I saw I was standing in quicksand! I shouted for my sisters to come save me, but they just kept on doing their stunts. Meanwhile I could feel myself getting sucked down . . . down . . . down. So I hollered even louder. Then Mo looked over at me and said . . .

"Is she okay?"

I sat up with a yelp. Three shapes were outlined against the sun. As I blinked my eyes into focus, I saw that it wasn't Darby, Delaney, and Mo peering back at me, but Jay, Robbie, and Nelson.

"Nelson thought you were dead," Robbie said.

"Nuh-uh!" Nelson elbowed Robbie. "I said I thought she was dying. She was making funny sounds."

"What are you doing?" Jay asked me.

"I was resting, not that it's any of your business." I was feeling annoyed and embarrassed. Why did they turn up whenever I was in some sorry state?

I looked around and finally spotted the rest of my group out on the water. Their canoes were pointed toward the middle of the lake, so they probably hadn't noticed that the boys had joined me.

"We're on our expedition," Nelson said. "Which means we're exploring and —"

"I know what an expedition is!" I snapped. I could feel the heat rising inside me again. "You make it sound so important. Like you're on some sort of mission."

"Yeah, well, you wouldn't understand. We're just out cherishing the natural wonders, like Theodore Roosevelt said to do," Jay said.

"He was our twenty-sixth president of the United States," Nelson said.

I made a sound that was similar to a roar and jumped to my feet. "No. Oh no. You did *not* just tell me who Teddy Roosevelt was!"

Nelson took a step back, his eyes as big as tennis balls.

"I'm so tired of you guys acting like you know everything. Guess what? We know all kinds of stuff. Tons of it. We can name all fifty states and their capitals in alphabetical order. We can name all of the U.S. presidents and vice presidents in chronological order. We can recite all the Constitutional amendments and the Gettysburg Address by heart. We even have meetings and make decisions using a democratic process. So don't keep saying 'you wouldn't understand' because know what? We do!"

The heat was taking over. In the back of my mind I started to wonder if I might burst into flames. Then I really would have to go jump in the lake — no matter how many toothy creatures might be in there.

For a moment, no one spoke. Then Robbie said, "Really? You guys hold meetings, too?"

"That's what I said. And I should know because I call them to order and preside over them!" I was proud to finally reveal my role as leader.

"Jay heads up our meetings," Robbie said. He and Nelson kept looking from Jay to me and back again.

"Oh yeah?" I said, putting my hands on my hips. "Well, we've probably been doing it longer than you guys. We probably do it better than you guys."

"Prove it!" Nelson said.

"I will!" I said, lifting my chin. Then I paused. "I just don't know how yet."

That's when Jay stepped forward. "I have an idea," he said.

CHAPTER ELEVEN

Citizenship

Darby

The canoes weren't as much fun as we'd hoped.

After we put on the bright yellow life vests that were lying in the canoes, it cost some effort to shove off from the beach. Delaney and I took one, with her sitting in front and me in the back, and Aunt Jane took another. Once we got them out on the water, we carefully climbed in, picked up the paddles, and headed out onto the lake.

It wasn't easy figuring out how to steer. At first Delaney and I couldn't get into a good rhythm, so we mainly went in circles. Eventually, we ended up in the middle of the cove and stopped paddling.

Aunt Jane said *"Ahh"* and just sat there, staring out at the scenery. I did the same and for a while, all I could hear was the slap of the water against our canoe and the calls of nearby birds. It was peaceful-lazy. Only Delaney must have gotten bored. She peered over the side, trying to see fish. This made the boat rock in an alarming way.

"Don't do that, Delaney!" I hollered. "You're going to tump us."

Delaney sat up straight and then slowly slid down onto the floor of the boat. "I just need to stretch out my legs."

"Fine. As long as you stay still," I said.

Delaney leaned back against her bench and let her arms dangle over the sides of the canoe. "You're right that this is fun, Aunt Jane," she said. "I mean, it was hard to get it in the water and get going, but I like it."

"They used to dock the boats," Aunt Jane explained. "But I guess they can't do that anymore." She nodded toward the wooden dock that, because the lake had partially dried up, was now almost completely on land.

"Why don't they build a new dock?" I asked.

Aunt Jane shrugged. "My guess is that they don't have the funds. Not as many people come here to camp, so there isn't as much money for upkeep and improvements."

"But wouldn't more campers come if there were fun things to do?" Delaney asked. "Like horse rides and boating?"

"I suppose so. It's a real catch-22."

"What's a catch-22?" I asked. I imagined it had to do with fishing. Maybe if you catch twenty-two fish it was bad luck?

"It means a can't-win situation. Mrs. Kimbro can't make improvements unless the campground earns more money, but the campground is losing money because she can't make improvements. It's like a trap she can't get out of." Aunt Jane stared off into the distance and looked mournful. It made me want to swim over to her boat and give her a hug. She really loved this place, and I was convinced more than ever that seeing it grow shabby was giving her the blues.

"Well, if I had lots of money, I'd give it to Mrs. Kimbro to help her fix up the campground and build a new dock," I said.

"Me too!" Delaney said. "Then she could get more horses. Maybe even a paint horse. Oh! And another dog for Mo."

"That's very kindhearted of you gals," Aunt Jane said.

"I bet Dawn would give some money, too," Delaney said.

"Oh yeah?" Aunt Jane raised her eyebrows. "I wonder what specific improvements she'd want."

Delaney and I both stared up at the sky, thinking.

"I know!" I said. "They could put in zip lines in the trees! That way people could get around off the ground and avoid fire ants."

Aunt Jane laughed. "Now there's an interesting idea. I know Dawn would like steering clear of ants, but I'm not sure she'd go for the zip lines. That sounds more like a Darby fantasy."

"As long as we're talking fantasy fix-ups," Delaney said, "I wouldn't mind building a whole zoo in addition to horse rides."

"With unicorns and winged horses!" I said.

"And whangdoodles!" Aunt Jane added.

We really cracked up at that one. Delaney did her wiggly laugh and, again, almost capsized the canoe. It was around then that I realized my feet were wet.

"We're leaking!" I called out. "There's water coming in at the bottom." It wasn't even covering my feet yet, but it was way more water than the accidental splashes from paddles could bring in. I patted around with my fingers, and found water seeping in at one of the seams.

"Hey! My rear end is all wet!" Delaney cried out, leaping to her feet.

The movement made the boat rock wildly. I heard Aunt Jane say, "Delaney don't —!" and then *SPLASH!* I was suddenly in the lake.

Even though the life jacket was keeping me afloat, I still got a little water up my nose. I could hear Delaney sputtering on the other side of the upside-down canoe.

"Sorry," she called out.

"That's okay," I reassured her. "With that leak, we might have ended up this way no matter what."

"You girls all right?" Aunt Jane asked, paddling up closer. We nodded.

"No sense trying to flip it over," she said. "We're not far from the beach, so let's just push it back."

We retrieved our paddles and put them in Aunt Jane's

boat. After quite a bit of effort, we eventually pointed our canoe in the direction of the beach. Delaney and I dogpaddled beside it, giving it little pushes. Aunt Jane paddled close behind, also pushing with her hands and oar.

As we came closer to shore, I could see Dawn standing on the banks of the lake talking with Jay, Robbie, and Nelson. She had her hands on her hips and her chin was raised up so high the boys could probably stare up her nostrils.

I had a sinking feeling — and not just because our boat had been sinking.

Eventually, we reached shallower part and my feet hit bottom. Aunt Jane got her boat onto shore and then, with her help, we turned our canoe sideways and slowly dragged it onto the bank.

"What happened to you guys?" Dawn asked, running up to us. The boys, I noticed, were already gone.

"Our boat had a hole and started taking on water," Delaney explained as she unhooked her life vest. "Then we fell in. But it was kind of exciting."

"You gals stay here while I go tell Tammy about the leaky canoe," Aunt Jane said. "And if you get tired or want to dry off, just go on back to the trailer."

"Aye-aye, Captain Aunt Jane." Dawn was grinning. She seemed awfully cheerful. For some reason, this made me nervous.

As soon as Aunt Jane jogged off toward HQ, Dawn clapped

her hands together and said, "So I guess y'all should know, I entered us in a competition."

"What kind of competition?" Delaney asked.

"We're going to see who is best at running a camping team — the three of us or those braggart boys." Dawn started pacing the beach.

I was confused — and still feeling uneasy. "I don't get it. A competition over . . . what?"

"Our respective governmental systems," Dawn said. "Who does things best — them or us? Of course it's us."

"O-kay . . ." I still wasn't clear. "But how does that work? Are we supposed to just have meetings and see who has the best ones?"

"That doesn't sound like fun," Delaney said.

"Don't be silly," Dawn said with a wave of her hand. "We agreed to do camping challenges. After three, whichever group is ahead wins!"

She sure seemed different. Just a few hours ago Dawn was a pitiful sight — all pink-faced and screeching about going home. Now she was calm and smiling a catlike smile. I wasn't sure which Dawn made me more anxious.

"What kind of challenges?" I asked.

"Well, first off, each team needs to come up with their own flag. That was my brilliant idea. The other two contests will be decided on later. We didn't have a lot of time to plan it, so we're going to meet up tomorrow in the Neutral Zone — and we'll bring our new flags." She clapped three times and gestured toward the trail. "So come on. Let's head back to the camper."

"Fine," I said with a shrug. "I guess our fun here is done for the time being. And I wouldn't mind changing into dry clothes."

"Yeah, and maybe we'll find Mo on the way!" Delaney said excitedly.

As we headed back to our campsite, Dawn told us about running into the boys, how they'd made her mad, and how Jay had suggested the camping challenge. I still wasn't entirely sure what we'd be doing, but I figured it couldn't be too bad. Besides, I love playing games.

We reached the trailer without seeing Mo, but Delaney found a ladybug that helped take her mind off of it. We made her release it before we went inside.

Delaney and I quickly changed into dry clothes while Dawn tapped her foot and told us to hurry. Whatever Aunt Jane had been doing that morning while we cooked breakfast was still on the table — a pen and a small notepad with lots of numbers on it. I placed both things on top of her bag and sat down on the padded bench.

In front of me stood the empty soda bottle holding the flowers Aunt Jane picked. They were all drooped over, their petals looking saggy and puny.

I always feel bad for picked flowers. I imagine they miss being outside where they belong. Today I could really relate.

"Just think. Our own flag!" Delaney hopped up and down on the bench beside me, making my view of the sad flowers bounce. "And we already have a motto. I bet those boys don't have a motto."

There was a drawer in the camper that held maps and tools and other important stuff. Dawn opened it and began rummaging around.

"Here," she said, setting a stack of blank paper and a box of pens, pencils, and markers on the tabletop between us. "Let's sketch out some ideas. Once we have a good design, we can copy it onto this." She held up an old extra pillowcase. "I'm sure Aunt Jane won't mind."

I glanced longingly out the window. "Do we have to do it now? It's so nice outside."

"Yeah. And Mo is somewhere out there, all lonely," Delaney said.

"We can romp around any old time, but this is real and important business," Dawn said. She sat down at the table and handed us each a piece of paper. "No one leaves until we have ourselves a perfect Brewster Team flag."

I let out a long sigh. It was good to see that Dawn got her moxie back. I just wish she'd returned to normal moxie instead of extreme moxie.

"Our flag shouldn't be too crazy," Dawn went on as she took her place on the padded bench. "Mainly it needs a symbol. Some sort of object or plant or animal."

"I know!" Delaney sat up ramrod straight. "How about a donkey?"

"Delaney, that's taken — remember? They'll think we stole it from the Democratic Party." Dawn tapped the side of her chin with a purple pencil. "Our symbol should be something that is meaningful to us in particular."

"A bobcat!"

"Except we haven't actually seen one of those here," Dawn said. "Same with horses."

"Probably not ants either — right?" Delaney asked.

Dawn's expression was about equal to a long angry rant, but much quicker.

"Let's all draw up some ideas. Remember that it should represent us and our family. And keep in mind" — she looked at Delaney — "it doesn't have to be an animal."

For a while it was quiet. No one spoke and I could only hear the scratching sounds of pen against paper.

I sat twirling a green marker in my hand, trying to think. What sort of thing would be associated with us? A crooked camper? A leaky boat? Wilted flowers?

I gazed out the window again at the grass and trees and flying insects. And just then, I got an idea. I reached forward, grabbed a handful of markers, and started drawing,

Just as I was putting on the finishing touches, Dawn said, "All right. Let's check on everyone's progress. Who wants to share their flag design?"

"I've got a good one!" Delaney held up her drawing. It was basically a brown mound with lines emanating off of it — as if it were shiny, like the sun.

Dawn squinted at it. "Um . . . I'm kind of afraid to ask but . . . what is it?"

Delaney looked confused. "Chocolate?"

"Ohhh. I thought it was . . . something else," Dawn said.

"It's our Daily Chocolate! That has to do with us, right?"

"I like that you kept it original, Delaney, but . . . uh . . . I don't think people are going to look at it and see chocolate."

Delaney frowned down at her drawing. Then her eyebrows rose up. "Oh," she said. "Never mind." She set her drawing facedown on the table. "What about you, Dawn? What symbol did you come up with?"

Dawn looked sheepish. "I actually didn't get a good idea." We glanced at her paper and saw it was just a bunch of crossed-out shapes.

"How about you, Darby?" Delaney asked. They both gazed at me, their faces full of hope.

"Well . . ." I grinned and held up my sketch. "It's a branch. See? It starts off big at the bottom and then splits off into three twigs with leaves. Three twigs for the three of us. Also, it represents the three branches of government — executive, judiciary, and legislative."

I set it down in the middle of the table so they could see it better. This way they could also see where I put our motto "United in Fun" in colorful letters across the top. In the lower left-hand corner I'd put "Lake Lewis," and in the lower right-hand corner I'd written "Campsite 19."

I bit my lip and waited for their reactions.

For a while all they did was squint down at it, and I worried maybe they didn't like it.

"Darby Brewster, that is the most beautiful flag design I've ever seen," Dawn said. "Second only to the stars and stripes. We have ourselves a winner!"

CHAPTER TWELVE

Checks and Balances

Delaney

They said they'd meet us here at daybreak," Dawn said. "If day broke anymore it would be lunchtime."

We were standing in the Neutral Zone — the area between the two campsites where we'd first seen Jay, Robbie, and Nelson. Dawn told us the boys had agreed to meet us at sunrise so we could present our flags and review the rules of the competition. Only we were here, and they weren't.

"Maybe they changed their mind about the contest?" Darby said.

I sort of hoped that was the case, and sort of didn't. On the one hand, it would be great to go back to regular camping and relaxing. On the other hand, if the boys backed out, Dawn would probably insist on calling it quits at the campground. Then I might never see Mo again.

"You guys, I feel bad that Aunt Jane is going to wake up and find us gone," Darby said.

"We left a note explaining," Dawn said.

She was sort of right. We'd written that we went to a club meeting with some other campers. That wasn't a complete lie, but it wasn't the truth, either.

"We trust Aunt Jane," I said. "So why do we have to keep our challenge with the boys a secret?"

Dawn let out a loud sigh. "I know. But why add to her worries when we want to cheer her up? Besides, she might not understand the competition. To her, it might seem like asking for trouble — like poking a wasp nest with a stick."

I thought that was a good point.

"Besides, it looks like the boys forgot about it," Darby said.

"Delaney, you're the speediest one of us," Dawn said. "Can you hop over to their campsite and find out where they are?"

"Sure." I pushed through the branches until I stepped into a part grass, part gravel clearing, just like our campsite. Parked on the opposite side from me was a big RV. It was white with blue stripes and had a satellite dish on the roof. Light was flickering inside it.

I knocked, and there came the sounds of muffled voices and feet thumping. Eventually, the door opened and I found myself looking at a tall, bearded man with long bushy hair.

"Well, good morning," he said, smiling at me.

"Hello. I'm here to see Jay, Robbie, and Nelson."

"Roberto, you boys have company," he called over his shoulder. I looked past him into a small living room area. The flickering light had come from a TV screen mounted on the wall. Robbie stood up from a cushioned bench and joined us at the doorway.

"Where are Jayden and Nelson?" the bearded man asked him.

"They went to get provisions. They'll be back soon," Robbie said. Then he looked at me. "Hey. You're early."

I shook my head. "It's sunrise. I'm on time."

"Would you like to come in and watch TV?" the man asked me. "We're learning how to make crepes." He opened the door wide and stepped aside to make a pathway.

"No, thanks. My sisters are waiting for me, so I should get back." I turned to go.

"Hold up. I'll come with you," Robbie said. "Be back in a little while," he said to the bearded man and shut the camper door behind him.

"Who was that?" I asked as we headed toward the Neutral Zone.

"Our dad."

"Wait —" A tiny thought blew up big in my brain, like a popcorn kernel. "You mean you guys are brothers? I thought you three were just friends or in the same scout troop or something."

"I know, I know." Robbie's voice sounded tired all of a sudden. "People are always surprised because we don't look alike. All three of us are adopted. None of us are related by blood, but we're still family."

"What's it like? Being adopted?"

He shrugged. "I don't know. It's great. I mean, it's my life. I don't know what else it could be like, because I've only had my life."

"Yeah. People always ask us what it's like to be a triplet. But it's just how it is. You can't compare when you've only had one experience. I apologize for asking such a boneheaded question."

"It's okay." He lifted a shoulder as if he were shrugging the whole thing off. "That's how you learn things, right? By asking questions?" He looked right at me and grinned.

I realized I liked his eyes. They were so large it made me wonder if he could see more than most folks. Plus, the dark brown irises against the white made me think of paint horses — my favorite type.

Suddenly, Robbie stopped walking and looked nervous.

"What's wrong?" I asked, also coming to a stop. I glanced around, but didn't see anything dangerous.

"Can I ask you a favor?" he asked in a hushed voice.

"Um . . . sure."

"Please don't tell my brothers I was watching TV, okay? I mean, I wasn't really. I was just in there with Dad."

"I won't."

"Thanks," he said, letting go his breath as if he'd been holding it. "If Jay and Nelson find out, they'll accuse me of ignoring orders."

His words reminded me so much of Dawn. I pivoted around so he wouldn't see me smile and think I was making fun of him. But when I turned, I saw something leaning against the picnic table that made my smile go away.

"I promise I won't say anything about the TV," I assured him. "But can you answer a question for me? Has Nelson been killing rabbits with that bow and arrow?"

Robbie laughed. "It's not even real. The arrow tips are rubber. It could probably bruise someone or poke an eye out, so he does have to be careful. Mainly he just likes to act out all the Robin Hood movies he's watched. Our parents like to support our imaginations."

"They sound like good parents."

"They are. Mom teaches psychology at a college, which is how she knows so much about imaginations. They have a different spring break, so she couldn't come with us."

"What does your dad do?"

"He works in a restaurant. He's the best cook in the world!" Robbie sure seemed different than before. I'd been used to seeing him stand behind Jay, all quiet and slump-shouldered, but now he was grinning proudly and making big gestures with his hands. "Sometime during the break Dad's going to teach me how to make zucchini bread."

"Vegetables in bread? Yuck!"

"No, it's good. And Mom showed us how to play all kinds of card games."

This made me bounce a little, because we love card games, too. "Is she teaching you guys Spite and Malice?" I asked.

Robbie looked shocked. "No way. My mom's a really nice person."

"Oh, no, it's a card game," I said, giggling. "It's our favorite one."

"Oh." He started chuckling with me. "You know," he said, "I like your laugh. It's bouncy. Like you."

For some reason, this made my face go tingly. I laughed some more and listened to myself, trying to hear what he heard. Before I knew it, I couldn't stop. My laughter got higher and faster and louder. That's when Robbie's big brown eyes started to look a little worried.

Just then we heard someone shout, "Hey!" We both jumped. Robbie made a tiny *"Eep!"* sound and I swallowed all my laughter back down inside me.

Jay and Nelson were jogging up behind us from the road.

"Where are y'all going?" Nelson asked.

"To the meeting at the Neutral Zone," I replied. "Where have you guys been?"

"We had to get supplies," Jay said. He was carrying a big duffel-type bag and the backpack he had on looked stuffed full. "What have you been up to?" he asked Robbie.

"Nothing. Just waiting." Robbie's shoulders hunched and his voice went low and mumbly. Probably he was worried I might tell about the TV. But of course, I wouldn't.

I studied Jay, Robbie, and Nelson as we all headed toward the Neutral Zone. It made me wonder which was harder — to have siblings who looked exactly like you, like I did, which made people mix you up all the time, or siblings that looked really different from you, like Robbie had, which made people think you didn't go together at all.

Jay and Robbie had hair that was almost the same color, only Jay's lifted off his head in tight curls while Robbie's was straight and sat on his head like an upturned bowl. Unlike Robbie's wide, wondering eyes, Jay's eyes were narrower and always seemed to be analyzing things.

The first time I met Nelson, he reminded me of someone, but it took me a while to figure out who. Now I realized that he looked just like a Hummel figurine Mom had back home in her room — of a little boy with a basket of playful white rabbits. He had the same orange-colored hair, rosy cheeks, and bright green eyes.

Only I would never trust Nelson with a basket of rabbits.

"About time!" Dawn said as the four of us reached the meeting spot. Her arms were folded across her chest and her right sneaker was tapping against the gravel.

"Sorry," I said. "It took a while to track them all down."

We all sat down on the ground — not exactly in a circle, more like a happy-face shape. Dawn and Jay sat near each other on one side and the rest of us sat in a curve facing them.

"Everyone set?" Jay asked. "Good. I officially call us to order."

"And *I* call *us* to order," Dawn chimed in.

"Before we get started, we should review the rules of the competition." Jay turned his head, meeting each of our gazes. "Does anyone here have questions?"

I thought this was a nice touch, and I made a mental note to ask Dawn to add this to our meetings.

"I do," I said, raising my hand.

"The chair recognizes . . . what's your name?" Jay asked.

"*This* chair actually recognizes her," Dawn said kind of snippily. "Go ahead, Delaney."

I cleared my throat. "So what is this competition all about anyway?"

Dawn scowled as if she thought I should know this. Jay opened his mouth to speak, then looked over at Dawn. "May I?" he asked. I thought this was another nice touch.

Dawn nodded.

"Yesterday at the lake we agreed to have a contest," Jay said, "to see which group is the most cohesive, the best governed, and therefore the most effective at camping."

"That's easy. We're the best!" Nelson said.

"The chair does not recognize the rude red-headed kid whose name I forget!" Dawn snapped. She waited to see if Nelson was going to say anything more. When he didn't, she turned to Jay. "You may continue."

"Basically," Jay went on, "we'll have a series of three agreed-upon challenges. The group that wins the most will be considered best."

"Challenge number one . . . team flags!" Dawn reached behind her and pulled out our flag. "Behold, fellows. Ours is a clear winner."

"Nice," Robbie said. "Very balanced." I could see Nelson give him the stink eye.

"Yes, fine job. But . . ." Jay reached into his backpack and pulled out a rolled-up towel. "Ours, I think, is superior." With a small flourish, he unrolled the towel and held it up for all to see.

I had to admit it was impressive. Their symbol was three hands, one a light tan, one a medium brown, and one a slightly darker brown, all holding on to one another at the wrist to make a triangle shape. The drawing was beautiful — it was even carefully shadowed so that it looked more lifelike.

"Wow," I exclaimed. Darby also went "Ooh!" When Dawn gave us an annoyed look, Darby said, "What? Hands are hard to draw."

"Robbie did it," Nelson said. "He's awesome at drawing."

Robbie smiled shyly and looked down at his lap.

"So . . . how do we decide the winner?" I asked.

"Maybe we should use an independent judge," Darby said. "Someone not in this group."

Nelson scrambled to his feet. "I'll go get Dad."

"Hold up there, mister," Dawn said. "Judges should be neutral. So not any of our relatives. Someone else."

"I agree," Jay said. "But who?"

We all kind of shifted around for a few seconds, then Darby raised her arm in that shy halfway up, halfway down way of hers.

"The chair recognizes Darby," Dawn said.

"Why don't we ask Mrs. Kimbro to judge?" Darby said. "She's nice."

Everyone agreed that this was the best idea so far, and no one seemed to have any other suggestions.

"Great," I said. "Let's go!" I started to stand up.

"Wait. Before we close the meeting, we have one more item of business to discuss," Jay said.

"What's that?" Robbie asked.

"Our second challenge." Jay reached behind him and grabbed the big duffel bag I'd seen him carrying earlier. "I think lodging should be next. I propose that each group sets up their own camping shelter. Then we can have somebody judge which is better."

"Would we have to sleep in the shelter, too?" I asked.

"Yes," Jay answered.

"Sounds good to me," Nelson said.

"The right thing to do," Dawn said, "is put it to a vote." Her chin was raised and her voice was confident, but I thought I heard a slight hesitation. I wondered if she was secretly hoping the proposal would fail.

But as it turned out, everyone said "aye," including Dawn — although she was the last one to say it.

"Great. Everyone sets up their shelter today and sleeps in it tonight to prove it will hold up. Then tomorrow we'll have the judging to see who did the best job," Jay said.

"And after that, we can move back into the RV?" Robbie asked.

"Why would we do that?" Jay replied. "It's a camping challenge, and real campers sleep in tents."

"Yeah. You aren't afraid, are you?" Nelson said to Robbie. He turned toward Jay, lowered his voice, and said, "I can keep the bow and arrow with me, right?"

"Ahem. I hate to repeat myself, but since this is not a monarchy and you are not the crowned king, I suggest we put that to a vote, too," Dawn said.

"Of course," Jay said, but he seemed a teensy bit miffed. He was probably used to bossing people around — just like Dawn was. Having two people preside over a meeting was weird. I could understand why we didn't have co-presidents in this country.

Again we voted and again the measure passed. Dawn and Robbie were the last ones to raise their hands.

"I guess it's settled then," Dawn said.

"Yep. Now it is," Jay said, clapping his hands together. "Time to end the meeting and decide who wins the flag contest."

Dawn also clapped her hands together. "Agreed."

"Meeting adjourned!" Jay and Dawn said quickly, as if trying to beat the other to it.

As we all got up to head to HQ and find Mrs. Kimbro, I caught Robbie's eye. He was back to looking stooped and bashful, so I gave him a thumbs-up sign to wish him luck. He smiled.

CHAPTER THIRTEEN

Flag Poll

Dawn

And so, the Great Camping Challenge was now officially underway.

After the meeting, the six of us headed directly to HQ to ask Mrs. Kimbro to choose the best flag. Jay and I kept trying to be in front, but without being obvious. I would walk faster in order to gain the lead, and then he'd speed up to pass me. He'd stretch his arms way out, pretending like he was exercising, to block my way. Then I'd bend over, pretending to check my shoelaces, so that I could duck under his arm. We ended up making it to HQ speedy quick. The only setback came when we passed Mo standing in a clump of trees and almost lost Delaney.

Mrs. Kimbro was so busy cooking breakfast and ringing up purchases of bait for the early-rising fishing folks that she seemed to have six arms. We waited patiently at the counter for our turn. Well . . . we might have looked just a little impatient. I drummed my fingertips on the countertop, Nelson kept sighing loudly, and Delaney was bouncing like a jump rope champion. But we weren't rude.

"Come on," Nelson muttered. "I bet Francis Scott Key didn't have to wait this long to show his flag design."

"You're thinking of Betsy Ross," Jay said. "Francis Scott Key wrote the national anthem."

"Actually," I said, "Francis Scott Key wrote a poem that was adapted into lyrics for 'The Star Spangled Banner.' And it didn't become our national anthem until the 1930s."

"When Herbert Hoover was in office," Jay said.

"Our thirty-first president," I added.

"For only one term," Jay added.

"Who was succeeded by Franklin Delano Roosevelt," I added.

"Who was elected four times," Jay added.

"Who actually only served three full terms since —" Only I didn't get to finish explaining. Because right at that moment, Mrs. Kimbro came up to us.

"Good morning!" she greeted me, Darby, Delaney, and Robbie. "And hello again to you two," she said to Jay and Nelson. "What can I do for all you young folks?"

"We're having a contest," Jay said. "Ma'am, would you mind judging these flags and declaring a winner? It shouldn't take too long."

"Well, now. I'm honored," she said, her smile growing even bigger. "I suppose I have enough time to do that."

We spread the two flags out side by side on the counter so that they were upside down to us, but right-side up for her.

"Hmm . . . Let's see . . ." she said. "Both are beautiful. This right here is a lovely sketch. Very realistic." She tapped the boys' flag with her index finger.

The boys got all puffed-up and proud-looking. I scowled.

"Whereas this one has a great use of color. And I like all the additional details." She indicated the motto across the top of our flag. "It isn't just a pretty picture, it's also a very effective design."

It was our turn to lift our chins in triumph.

"So that one's the winner, right?" I asked.

"No way!" Nelson said. "Look there where it's coming apart." He pointed to the top left corner where the fabric was starting to fray.

"That's not our fault," Darby said. "We had to make do with what we had on hand, so we had to cut up this old pillowcase. It's not like we have a sewing machine with us."

"Besides, you guys used a souvenir towel," Delaney pointed out. "You can see the outline of the Alamo that's on the other side."

Mrs. Kimbro shook her head. "Guys and gals, I'm sorry but I just can't choose between them. To me, it's a tie."

"But —" Nelson started to argue but she held up both hands.

"You asked my opinion and I've given it," Mrs. Kimbro said. "Now if you'll kindly excuse me, I have lots of work I need to do."

"Thanks, Mrs. Kimbro," Darby said. The rest of us added our thank-yous.

"You're welcome." Mrs. Kimbro grinned. "I'm so glad y'all are having fun."

"Well, now what?" I asked after she walked away. As much as I liked Mrs. Kimbro, I was sorely disappointed in her inability to see the superiority of our flag.

"Let's get another judge!" Nelson said, glancing around HQ.

"But it's binding," Delaney said. "We all agreed to abide by her decision."

"That's right. We can't change our rules just because we don't like the outcome," Darby said.

I bit my lip, feeling a little bit ashamed that I agreed with Nelson.

"We should move on to the second challenge," Jay said. "Tomorrow morning we'll see which group has set up the best shelter."

"We will!" Nelson said.

I stopped secretly agreeing with him and narrowed my eyes at him.

"It's probably time to get back," Robbie said. "Dad's making breakfast."

"We'll see you all tomorrow morning at the meeting place," Jay said before they all headed out the door and back down the path.

"Yeah," I called after them. "Tomorrow."

But tomorrow seemed ridiculously far off. I wanted to show up those boys now. I needed to prove what we were capable of, and I didn't want to wait.

CHAPTER FOURTEEN

Special Session

Darby

Delaney started skipping toward Camp HQ's exit, and I fell into step behind her.

"Hold up," came Dawn's voice from behind us. "Where are y'all off to so fast?"

"Back to the campsite?" Delaney looked confused.

Dawn shook her head. "Not yet. Let's have a quick team meeting. We need to decide our strategy for the next contest in the Great Camping Challenge. We can't afford to lose another."

"But we didn't lose this one," I pointed out.

Only Dawn didn't seem to hear me. She headed to one of the square wooden tables on the patio and waited for us to join her.

"Aunt Jane's going to be worried if we don't show up for breakfast soon," Delaney said. "Plus, Mo's probably waiting for us. Plus, I'm hungry."

"This won't take long." Dawn sat there with her chin raised and her hands folded on the tabletop in front of her. It was her best presidential look — calm and serious, but with a clear don't-mess-with-me stare.

Delaney and I didn't even risk glancing at each other before sitting down. Our sisterhood was a proud democracy, but we'd learned from experience that it was just better to hear Dawn out than try to argue with her. Besides, most of the time she had important stuff to say. Important to her anyway.

"We need to have a plan," Dawn began. "We can't agree to a shelter challenge and then spend the day romping with donkeys."

"There's just one donkey," Delaney pointed out.

"A plan for what exactly? All we need to do is get a tent and set it up, and we have the whole day to do that," I said.

"We have to prepare," Dawn said. "We should do some research and inspect other people's tents."

"But isn't that trespassing?" I asked.

Dawn paused and tapped her chin a couple of times. "I mean from afar, of course."

Delaney's legs started jiggling impatiently, and her feet made a sound like a drum roll — until Dawn's steely-eyed stare caused her to stop.

"I feel like one of us should be on alert at all times," Dawn went on. "Those boys might try to snoop or eavesdrop on us.

Also, we should try to snoop or eavesdrop on them if we get the chance."

"But what about, you know, having some fun today?" Delaney asked.

"*Fun?*" Dawn's forehead went wavy, and she pronounced the word like she didn't understand it — as if Delaney had asked about having *bloogletootie.*

"Yeah, fun," I repeated.

Dawn blew out her breath. "We can have *fun* any old time. Besides, what could be better than showing up those three boys?"

Delaney and I finally sneaked that glance at each other. We could list lots of things that would be more fun. We just weren't sure if we should.

"So come on," Dawn said. "Let's go rent a tent and set it up."

"But we haven't even had breakfast yet," Delaney said. "I'm sure Aunt Jane's up by now. She's all alone. And probably hungry. Like I am."

"Also, don't we need to ask Aunt Jane for permission? And money?" I added.

Dawn's mouth bunched up. "You have a point."

"We can keep an eye out for the boys while we spend quality time with Aunt Jane," I said.

"And we can study other tents while we play with Mo and do other fun stuff," Delaney said.

"Come on, Dawn," I pleaded. "We want to do well in the challenge. But we also want to spend time with Aunt Jane and make her happy. She's most important — right?"

"I guess you're right," Dawn said.

"Yay!" Delaney jumped up from the table.

"But!" Dawn blurted, making Delaney pause. "We still have lots of stuff to do, so how about we spend the morning and lunchtime with Aunt Jane and focus on our challenge in the afternoon?"

"That sounds fair," I said.

"Deal," Delaney said.

We headed off, pausing to wave at Mrs. Kimbro who was still bustling around. Outside, the sun was now over the treetops.

"Come on!" shouted Dawn, who was already several steps ahead of us.

"You go on ahead!" Delaney shouted back. "I'm looking for Mo!"

I started jogging to catch up when suddenly Delaney grabbed my arm. "Wait!" she said. "We need to have an emergency meeting."

"But . . . we just had a meeting."

"I know but we need to have another. We need to have an emergency meeting *about Dawn*."

"Huh?"

"Dawn is going to ruin the whole trip," she said. "First she says she hates it here, but now she's being super competitive with those boys. She doesn't even want us to have fun."

I had to agree that Dawn's sudden change made me feel wobbly. "Yeah. She wants to stay just to win the Great Camping Challenge. But the thing is . . . I also want to stay. I like it here at the campground with Aunt Jane. If this is the only way we can get Dawn to stop bellyaching and give this place a chance, I'm all for it. Do you want to go home?"

"No," Delaney said, digging the toe of her sneaker into the pebbly dirt. "I just don't want this contest to take over everything."

I watched as Dawn strode down the trail ahead of us in that purposeful way of hers — head raised high, arms swinging beside her. "I think Dawn needs something to focus on," I said. "She's been all out of sorts here. Remember how she was fretting over silly stuff like us walking on the fence?"

Delaney nodded. "She even seemed afraid of the canoes." Her gaze turned thoughtful. "Which I guess was pretty smart of her, considering what happened."

"So . . . we're agreed?"

"Agreed," Delaney said, and we shook hands. "Although," she added, "I still think Dawn's a little bonkers."

Dawn was waiting for us on the trail. "You two sure are poky."

"That's because we need nourishment," Delaney said.

We hurried back to the campsite and found that Aunt Jane was awake. She was already washing a bowl in the rubber dishwashing tub, so it seemed like she'd been up for a while.

"Good morning, girls. Thank you for leaving another note," she said. "How was your meet up with the other kids?"

"Fine," Dawn said.

"Any of you hungry?"

"Delaney could probably eat a horse," I said.

"I'd never eat a horse!" Delaney gasped. "I am hungry, though."

"Well, good. I made oatmeal and chopped up a couple of apples to put on top." Aunt Jane gestured to a covered pot and a few bowls on the picnic table. "I hope you girls don't mind, but I'm headed off to HQ to help Tammy. I hate to see how shorthanded she is, and I want to see what I can do for this old campground." She finished drying her dish, set it with the others, and started jogging toward the edge of our campsite. "Y'all come join me when you're done and we'll have some fun. See ya!"

Delaney and Dawn immediately started serving themselves breakfast — Delaney slipping chopped apples in her pocket for Mo. Meanwhile, I watched as Aunt Jane's brown curls disappeared amid the trees.

"Aw, man. Now what?" I said. "We were going to spend our morning cheering up Aunt Jane."

"Oh well. Guess we should research tent making after all," Dawn said.

"No!" I whined. "We have to do something. Didn't you see how mopey she looked when she was talking about the campground?"

"Yep. She was gloomy," Delaney said with her mouth full of oatmeal.

Dawn sighed. "You're right, but . . . how can we cheer her up if she isn't here?"

Just then, a terrible racket came from the nearby bushes. It sounded like a wheezy bugle call. We all jumped — and then Delaney broke out in a huge grin.

"Mo's here! He's back!" She hopped up from the table and began a celebratory dance as Mo emerged from the brush and walked toward us.

"Hold on a minute . . ." A plan was starting to materialize in my mind. It took a while for it to come into focus, but suddenly it was clear and colorful and high definition. "I've got it! I really got it! I know how we can help the camp *and* cheer up Aunt Jane!"

Then I started dancing, too.

CHAPTER FIFTEEN

Public Works

Delaney

Step right up! Get your donkey rides right here! Meet Mo, the world famous ride-giver donkey, at your service!" I was standing in the field down the hill from Camp HQ, calling out to any campers who might be nearby. Mo stood on one side of me and Dawn stood on the other.

Meanwhile Darby was stationed near the road holding up our homemade paper sign that read:

INCREDIBLE DONKEY RIDES!
Fun! Not-Scary-Fast! Reasonable Prices!
Line Starts HERE

The campground couldn't afford to offer horse rides anymore. But now they were in danger of losing business because they don't have many exciting activities.

Except for donkey rides! We figure with this new offering

we could liven up the camp, make money for Mrs. Kimbro, and cheer up Aunt Jane. It was a brilliant idea.

Only . . . for some reason no one was lining up yet. So far two campers had walked past on their way from HQ, but they just smiled at us and kept going.

"Maybe we should give up and build our shelter," Dawn said.

"No!" I said. "It's not even lunchtime yet. We have plenty of time to lure customers."

"People probably aren't hearing you," Dawn said. "If the camp had a loudspeaker system, it would solve everything. Perhaps we can help them raise money for that, too."

I cupped my hands around my mouth again and yelled out, "Donkey rides! Right here! Get your enjoyable, inexpensive donkey rides! Lots of fun from four feet off the ground!"

Finally, a boy came up the trail toward us. He looked confused. "Is that the incredible donkey?" he asked, pointing at Mo.

I patted Mo's haunches proudly. "He sure is."

He tilted his head and looked Mo over. "Okay. I'll ride him. How much is it?"

I suddenly realized I'd been so focused on getting a customer, I'd completely forgotten the rates.

"One second while I consult my business partner." I leaned over and whispered in Dawn's ear, "How much did we decide?"

"How old are you?" she asked the boy.

"Six."

"That'll be one dollar."

The boy pulled a dollar out of his shorts pocket and handed it to Dawn. Then she and I gave him a small boost and helped him climb onto Mo's back.

"So what now?" he said. "Do I say giddyap?"

I shook my head. "No. Mo doesn't actually understand that language."

"How do I make him move?"

"Well, you don't really," I said. "You just sit on him and wherever he wants to go, you go with him."

"It's a ride-along kind of ride," Dawn added.

For a moment, it looked like Mo just wanted to stay put. He took tiny steps here and there and sniffed the air and twitched his ears. It was adorable, but I could tell the boy was getting bored.

Finally, Mo started walking. "Oh, look. Here he goes. Hang on tight," I said. "He's heading into a shady spot. We're passing a tree. Now we're passing another tree. You can't see it but he's flicking his tail — probably to shoo away some bugs. Now we're at his favorite special bush."

"What's so special about it?" the boy asked.

"Well, obviously it tastes good."

The boy sighed. "I want to get down now."

"Probably a smart idea," I said. "This is his favorite resting spot."

The boy slid down off Mo's back and ran down the road toward the campsites.

"Tell all your friends!" I called after him.

"Delaney," Dawn said. "I'm not sure these rides are the rip-roaring fun we hoped they'd be."

"How can you say that?"

"Because Mo only walked about five feet. And how thrilling can it be when we're able to walk along beside him at the same speed?"

"Don't listen to her, Mo," I whispered. "It's fascinating just being near you."

As I'd predicted, Mo knelt down in his usual napping spot with a grunt. I was proud of him for helping us out with our plan, and I could tell he was doing his best.

Just then, I heard footsteps and saw Darby trotting toward us. "Since Mo's taking a break can we take a break, too?"

"That's a premium idea," Dawn said.

"Yeah, okay," I said. "I guess we should let Mo rest up for the next round."

"Besides," Darby said, changing her walk to a skip, "I can't wait to tell Aunt Jane about our moneymaking endeavor. It'll cheer her right up!"

We headed into Camp HQ for a cold drink and to present Mrs. Kimbro with the earnings. Aunt Jane and Mrs. Kimbro were sitting at one of the tables talking and drinking ice tea.

"There they are!" Aunt Jane said as she spotted us.

Mrs. Kimbro turned around and grinned at us. "Well, hello there. What's going on with you three?"

"We have a surprise for you!" Dawn tried to set down the dollar with as much flourish as possible, but it kind of just lay there on the tabletop all crumpled looking.

Mrs. Kimbro seemed baffled. "Well, how nice. What's this for?"

"It's for you! We earned it for the campground," I said, hopping up and down. "We started a special activity. Show them, Darby."

Darby held up the sign so they could read it.

"Oh, girls. The things you three get up to. That's . . . that's . . ." Aunt Jane couldn't even talk. She just kept blinking her eyes and shaking her head.

"Incredibly thoughtful is what that is," Mrs. Kimbro finished for her.

"We're just glad you're happy," Darby said. "We did it for the campground — and for you."

Mrs. Kimbro reached out and patted Darby's arm. "The thing is, girls, even though your idea was clever and kind, we just can't offer donkey rides," she said. "If we do, I could get in trouble."

"In trouble?" I repeated.

She nodded. "I can't offer such a thing without the proper permits and insurance."

"Well, jiminy," Dawn said, crossing her arms. "That just goes against the whole American dream, doesn't it?"

I stopped hopping, my shoulders slouched, and I could feel my smile sliding down into a sad hound dog expression.

"We didn't mean to get you in trouble," Darby said in a remorseful voice.

"Yeah. Sorry," Dawn said.

"We'll stop offering rides," I said. "And Mo will, too."

"It's the thought that counts. And y'all's thought was the kindest I've seen in a long time." Mrs. Kimbro smiled a smile that made me feel light again.

"I'm very proud of you girls for trying to help," Aunt Jane said. "Now then. This dollar should be returned to its owner. Who gave it to you?"

Dawn held her hand up a few inches above her waist. "A blond six-year-old about yea high."

"That would be John Michael," Mrs. Kimbro said. "I'll put it toward his family's tab."

"Thanks," I said.

Aunt Jane patted a nearby bench. "Well, as long as you all are here, why don't you sit a spell? Is there anything you need? Sodas maybe?"

"Actually, there is," Dawn said. "We need to rent a tent."

"Hey, that rhymes!" I exclaimed. "Rent a tent! That's what I meant." I started singing a little song — until Dawn gave me a bug-eyed look.

"A tent? What for?" Aunt Jane asked.

"Um . . . We just want to have the full camping

experience," Dawn said. "You know, sleep under the stars. That sort of thing."

"Girls, I'm sorry to disappoint you again," Mrs. Kimbro said, "but I'm afraid I can't rent you a tent."

"But . . . why not?" Dawn asked. Her eyes were wide and her face was turning the color of skim milk.

Mrs. Kimbro shrugged helplessly. "I'm plumb out. Those friends you made flags with? I rented the last one to two of them this morning."

Dear Bree,

How has your spring break been going?

We've been camping, and there's been lots of hair-raising events. For example, today Dawn lost her mind.

We were trying to rent a tent to sleep in instead of our camper (it's a long story), only the campground was out of all of their tents. We think we were set up by other, somewhat evil campers (that's another long story). When Dawn heard the news, she marched out of Camp HQ and threw one of the biggest fits I've ever seen her throw. She hollered at trees and shook her fist at the sky and kicked gravel and even scared off Mo, our friend who's a donkey. Her face was the color of a bad sunburn and when she wasn't yelling, she made these ferocious-sounding noises that didn't even seem human. It was kind of fascinating -- even if it was scary.

She tried to go rail at the spiteful villains who put us in this predicament, but we blocked her path. For the past two hours, she's been sulking in the camper, and I decided to write you while Darby and I keep an eye on her. Darby pointed out that it's the longest letter I've ever written!

I have a feeling that things might get worse for us, so stay tuned for more. I know you like dramatic tales.

(Of course, we just might end up on the news.)

Take care! Your friend,
Delaney

CHAPTER SIXTEEN

Assembly

Dawn

Good evening, girls. I brought you something from Tammy."
I could see Aunt Jane's outline against the setting sun. She appeared to be carrying a big mound in her arms.

"You found us a tent?" I asked, hopping up from the picnic table.

Her silhouette nodded. "Tammy had it in the shed. It's an older model that they don't rent out anymore. But it should still work fine."

She dropped the bag on the ground near the picnic table, and it landed with a *whomp*. The noise sounded like a call to action — like a fist pounding or a foot stomp. For the first time in hours, I felt calm and focused.

"Thanks, Aunt Jane," Darby said.

"You're the best," Delaney said.

They both turned toward me.

"I can't even express how much this means to me," I said. "Thank you doesn't seem to cover it. But thank you." I was feeling mighty shamefaced over the big tantrum I threw earlier. It was tough to look people in the eye.

"You're welcome," Aunt Jane said. "I understand this is important to you. Here . . ." She bent over and started to undo the drawstring on the tent bag. "Let me show you how —"

"No!" I shouted. Everyone stared at me again. "Sorry. We have to . . . that is, we *want* to do it ourselves. If you help us, it will rob us of a valuable character-building experience."

Aunt Jane lifted her hands as if surrendering. "All righty, then. Can't argue with that."

"Don't hurt her feelings," Darby whispered. "Remember, she got us the tent, even though it means we move out of the trailer. She wanted to camp with us and now we're doing our own thing."

"We'll still visit you in the camper all the time," Delaney said loudly to Aunt Jane. "And you are welcome to visit us in our tent anytime. I mean, it's only fair, you spending money on the rent-a-tent."

"Actually, because it was an old, retired tent, she loaned it to us at no cost. So it's a lent-a-tent."

Delaney laughed.

Aunt Jane stood behind Delaney and mussed up her hair. "Tell you what," she said. "How about you three set up the tent and then come visit for a game of cards, deal? Ha! No pun intended."

"In tent-ed?" Delaney said.

The two of them guffawed, and Darby chuckled a little, too. I rolled my eyes.

"All right. You're on your own. I'm gone," Aunt Jane said, and headed back into the trailer.

Now it was just me, Darby, Delaney, and a big bag of tent. It lay there, still tied up in a drawstring cover, looking like a big blue-gray sausage.

"Hey, I know," Delaney said, hopping up from the table. "Maybe we can invite over Nelson, Jay, and Robbie for the card game?"

"Why would we do that?" I snapped. Sometimes, just when I really need Delaney to focus, she comes up with the most outlandish ideas.

"Because . . ." Delaney's eyes searched the sky as she stretched out the word. "No reason, really. I just thought it would be nice."

"It would be nice," Darby said.

I stood up from the table and put my hands on my hips. "I shouldn't have to remind you this, but those rogues are our opponents. Plus, they rented the last tent and didn't tell us. Lousy cheats."

"Maybe they didn't realize it was the last one," Darby said. "Besides, the game isn't all day and all night. Once we set up the tent, we'll be done until the judging."

I shook my head. "Still a bad idea. Fraternizing with the enemy would give them a chance to gather intel and possibly sabotage our efforts. Now let's get to work setting this thing up."

Dusk was coming on, and it was getting hard to see. But we still had the light of the stars, the half-moon, and the glow from the inside of the camper — plus a flashlight. I figured that should be enough for us to assemble the tent.

The first thing we decided to do was empty the bag and lay out the different pieces of equipment to make sure we had all the parts. I snatched up a faded paper with instructions and tried to figure out what was what.

"Jiminy, this thing is old," Delaney said. "I wouldn't be surprised if Davy Crockett slept in this tent."

We were used to newer, spring-loaded-type tents that had the poles sewn into the fabric already. This one had all kinds of extra stuff we hadn't seen before. Plus, it was all dirty and musty smelling, and there were a couple of cobwebs stuck to things.

"What do the directions say, Dawn?" Darby asked me.

I scanned the rumpled document in the yellow glow of the flashlight. "No idea. What's a ferrule?"

Darby and Delaney shrugged.

"Dang instructions!" I stamped my foot in frustration. "They don't make any sense. Like this one part where it says we need to put a fly on the tent. Isn't the whole point of having a tent so you can be away from flies and mosquitos and mountain lions?"

The three of us conferred again and, in a unanimous vote,

decided that asking Aunt Jane to identify the equipment we couldn't recognize would not be a violation of the challenge. So we gathered up the stuff and knocked on the door of the trailer.

Aunt Jane undid the latch and peered out. "Well, lookee here. It's the Brewster triplets. What have you three been up to lately?" she joked.

"Trying to understand written directions that go against all rules of logic and grammar," I grumbled as I stepped inside with Darby and Delaney. "Will you please help us?"

"I'll do my best," she said.

As we laid out or held up the different pieces, Aunt Jane explained that the big plastic-looking sheet was the ground cover, one was the actual tent, and one was a rain cover that went over the tent — otherwise known as a "fly." Next she told us that the poles had to be connected together and then pushed through holes in the tent. Once we had it raised up, we had to stake it into the ground at the corners using the big nail-looking things.

"You're much better than the instructions at explaining things," Delaney said as we packed everything back up.

"Why, thank you," Aunt Jane said. As we headed back outside she said, "Door's open. Come see me anytime!"

Now that we knew what was what, we had to find a good location for the tent. After some debate, we decided to set it up under an oak tree, not far from the picnic table. It encroached slightly on the grassy area where we did Morning Cartwheels, but not too much. From there we'd be able to see the camper from the doorway and the boys' campsite from the tent's back window — allowing us to detect a possible invasion before it happened.

Once we knew where the tent would go, I held up a flashlight while Darby and Delaney scoured the ground and tossed rocks and other pointy things into the bushes. Then Darby and Delaney took turns holding the light while we spread out the tarp and the tent on the ground, fastened the poles together, poked them through the right holes, and raised the whole structure.

Finally, it was done. If you can call slightly misshapen and leaning toward the left done. At least it was standing and seemed likely to stay that way for a while.

"We're going to lose," I said, looking over our handiwork.

"You don't know that," Delaney said. "The boys' tent might be falling down all the time. Or full of holes. Or . . . or . . . haunted!"

"Face it, team," I said with a sigh. "We did our best, but thanks to their underhandedness, it's impossible for us to win this challenge."

Darby peered at me. "Do you want to pull out of the competition?"

I scowled again at our lopsided, mildew-stained, sickly green-colored dwelling. Now both Darby and Delaney were staring at me anxiously. They were probably worried I'd pitch another fit.

"No," I said finally. "Brewsters don't quit. We might make mistakes and, um, might have an occasional outburst, but we don't give up."

"Good!" Delaney said, and clapped her hands.

"Besides," Darby said, passing the flashlight beam over the tent. "I like it. It has character — like it's been through lots of adventures."

We called Aunt Jane outside to see our handiwork and she pronounced it a fine-looking tent.

"You girls sure are bulldogged. It makes me proud," Aunt Jane said. "So! Y'all ready for a game of Spite and Malice?"

"Yes!" we all shouted.

We followed her into the trailer and sat around the slanted table. Aunt Jane dealt the cards as we sipped cartons of fruit punch and snacked on raisin-free trail mix. Although we started out all fired up, we faded quickly. Darby kept yawning and making mistakes. At one point I nudged Delaney's shoulder when she was taking a long time to make a move, and saw that behind her raised cards, her eyes were closed.

That's when we decided it was time for bed.

Aunt Jane stood in the camper doorway and watched as we stumbled out toward our freshly assembled tent. We crawled inside, zipped up the flap of the doorway, and stretched out on our sleeping bags with me in the middle.

"Good night," I said. "I'm sorry I was a fussbucket today."

"That's okay," Darby said.

"Poodle," Delaney mumbled in her sleep.

The last thing I remember hearing is Aunt Jane calling out, "Sweet dreams, triplets." I closed my eyes and that was all.

CHAPTER SEVENTEEN

Unrest

Darby

I like camping for lots of reasons. I like to lie on the bunk inside our camper and just listen. Back home, most of the outdoorsy sounds are drowned out by people sounds, but here it's the other way around. You hear the gurgling of the nearby creek and the rustle of trees and the heavy sighing of the wind. Plus there are birds. Lots and lots of birds that twitter and chirp and caw and shriek.

I can close my eyes and pretend that I live outdoors — that I'm a wild beast and this is my home. Only just when I start to really believe it and forget myself, I'll hear Delaney start jabbering or Dawn start fussing or Aunt Jane would turn on the portable radio she likes to camp with . . . and I go back to feeling like regular old me.

I figured staying in a tent instead of a camper would make my dreams about being in the wild even more vivid, but last night I could barely sleep. I turned every which way — as much as I could in the cramped space — only nothing helped. It was as if I were lying on top of a boulder. It made it impossible to relax and drift off. Eventually, though, I must have.

"Knock, knock," called out Aunt Jane. "You three at home?"

My heavy eyelids opened a crack and I saw that our tent was bright with daylight. I felt a squeeze in my chest, as if my heart was wailing in protest. How could it be morning already?

"We're here!" cried Delaney. She sat up, spun around, and unzipped the door so that Aunt Jane could poke her head in.

"Let's see . . . one, two, three," Aunt Jane said pointing at each of us. "Good. All present and accounted for. Y'all ready for some grub?"

"Yes!" Delaney exclaimed.

"Good. Come out when you're ready." Aunt Jane's head disappeared from the tent opening.

I wondered if we should offer to make breakfast again, but after our results the other day, I wasn't sure it was really helpful. Besides, I was too tired to even open my mouth and suggest it.

Dawn and Delaney were crawling all around, rolling up their sleeping bags and jostling me every few seconds.

"Get moving, Darby," Dawn said. "We need to get this place ready for judging."

I tried to say "all right," but it came out sounding like "*awwwruh.*" Luckily, Dawn was bustling around so much, she didn't even hear it. Plus, Delaney was humming the *1812 Overture* for some reason, complete with explosion sounds.

"I'm going to get the small broom and dust pan. You guys keep picking up the place." Dawn scrambled out of the tent.

I tried to kick my sleeping bag off me, but it just kept getting tangled up in my legs. After the third try, I finally got free of it and sat up. My head was foggy and my eyelids felt like they each weighed ten pounds. The best I could manage was to open my right eye halfway.

Delaney stopped humming and frowned at me. "You okay? You look kind of feeble."

I shook my head. "I'm a wreck. I just couldn't get comfortable on the ground. It feels like my back is all black-and-blue."

"What are you? The Princess and the Pea?" Delaney laughed at her own joke. Then she looked at me and stopped. "Sorry. You really do look run-down. Maybe you should go back to sleep."

"I can't rest here. And if I go sleep in the camper, Dawn will spit fire."

Just then Dawn crawled in and stood on her knees at the front of the tent. "Hey! What are you two doing just sitting around jabbering? We don't have much time!"

"See?" I said, low enough so that only Delaney could hear.

I folded over my sleeping bag and was about to roll it up, when I noticed something.

"Look! There's a big rock here, right where I was lying," I said, pointing toward a raised lump in the tent floor. It was oval and slightly bigger than my fist. "No wonder I could barely sleep last night!"

"Holy moly! That's huge!" Delaney exclaimed.

"Jiminy!" Dawn peered over Delaney's shoulder. "You slept on that?"

"Yep," I said. "And now I'm all beat up."

Dawn patted my back. "Sorry. But it's your own fault. You two were in charge of clearing the area. I just provided light."

"But we did a good job. I don't know how we could have missed something so big." I poked the mound again, and suddenly, it wiggled. "Yipes!" I cried out in surprise. "The rock is moving!"

Sure enough it was heading toward the edge of the tent. I watched in wonder as the roundish shape inched itself along beneath the ground cover.

"Come on!" Delaney said. She scrambled out of the tent, followed by Dawn. By the time I caught up with them, they were crouched down outside the back of our tent.

"Hey, look. It's a little tortoise," Dawn said. She cupped her hands over her mouth and shouted, "Aunt Jane! Come see!" The volume of her voice hurt my sleepy head.

Aunt Jane came jogging over and stood with her hands

resting on her knees. "Well, lookee there," she said. "Where'd he come from?"

"Darby was sleeping on him," Dawn said.

"You poor thing!" Delaney exclaimed.

At first I thought Delaney was worried about me. Then I noticed that she was talking to the tortoise. She'd scooped him up in her hands and was patting him gently on his shell — which was the only part of him we could see now.

"Come on out, little guy. We won't hurt you," she crooned at the end of the shell where his head was hiding. "Let's see . . . what should we name you?"

"Delaney, you aren't seriously thinking about keeping him, are you?" Dawn asked.

"Why not?" Delaney said. "I can keep him in one of our empty boxes. I'll make sure he gets lots of food and water."

"That's a lousy idea. Just look at him. He's already hiding from us," Dawn said.

Delaney stroked the top of his shell. "He's just uncomfortable."

"He certainly is," I mumbled, rubbing a sore spot on my back.

"I'm afraid I agree with Dawn," Aunt Jane said. "We should let the tortoise go free — like Mo. Think how much happier that donkey is wandering around rather than being penned up."

Delaney looked thoughtful for a few seconds. "Fine," she

said finally. Then she set the tortoise down on the ground. After a moment, his head and legs reappeared and he started moving again. We watched him trudge into the bushes, slow and steady, as if he didn't have any bossy sisters telling him to hurry up.

"Bye, little guy!" Delaney called out. "See you around!"

"Sorry if I squished you!" I called out.

Aunt Jane stood up straight and clapped her hands together. "Well, I'm off to make those pancakes."

"Can I help?" Delaney asked.

"Why sure," Aunt Jane said.

"Yay!" Delaney said, doing a celebratory dance. "The great thing about making pancakes outside is there's no ceiling to mess up!"

They started to walk toward the picnic table, when suddenly Delaney came to a halt.

"Wait!" she said. "We should go do our Morning Cartwheels before we eat."

Aunt Jane grinned. "That's an excellent idea." She walked to the end of the grassy space. "All right now. Make room."

We stepped aside so that we wouldn't be in the way — and also to get a better view. Aunt Jane wheeled around almost perfectly this time. Her legs were straighter and she only wobbled a little. As we clapped, she took a little bow and then jogged off down the path.

Dawn went next, followed by Delaney.

Then it was my turn.

"I don't know about this," I said. "I don't feel all that great this morning."

"What are you talking about, Darby?" Delaney said. "You do cartwheels better than any of us. And I do them all the time."

"Yeah. You could probably do them in your sleep," Dawn said.

Since I was only about half asleep, I figured they were right. I walked over to the grassy area, lifted my arms, and whirled around.

Everything started okay, but midway through the "wheel" part, something went wrong. I heard my sisters yelling and everything went topsy-turvy. The sky whizzed past, then some trees, and finally I landed on my back. Surprisingly, it didn't hurt at all. In fact, it was kind of smooth and springy.

That's when I realized I had landed on the tent.

CHAPTER EIGHTEEN

Canvassing

Delaney

Hmmm . . ." Mr. Bartholomew squinted so hard at the boys' tent, his eyes seemed to disappear under his bushy eyebrows. Since his mouth was already hidden beneath his big gray mustache, his face looked like a nose surrounded by hair.

He certainly seemed to be taking his role as official tent judge very seriously — which was a good thing since we couldn't find anyone else. And even though the morning had been nutso, I was glad we were able to rebuild our tent in time and didn't have to forfeit.

I thought the boys' tent looked nice. Instead of triangular-shaped, it was a big dome with a little roof over the entrance. Their flag was pinned over their tent door like a banner and the flaps were wide open to show how tidy it was inside. It was so tall, you didn't have to hunch over to stand inside it.

Plus, it smelled new instead of old and didn't have any blotchy stains. It looked solid and livable — cozy even. Meanwhile, ours might have already been blown into the thicket by a strong wind.

We were going to lose.

Mr. Bartholomew slowly circled the tent, peering at it all over and even patting its bouncy nylon side. Meanwhile, Jay, Robbie, and Nelson stood in a line looking really pleased and proud. They also seemed to know they were going to win.

On one side of me stood Dawn with her chin raised up high. Her eyes kept scanning the clouds as if she were bored, but I wondered if maybe she just couldn't bear gazing at the boys' big, sturdy tent. Even though she looked puffed up with pride, I knew our mad scramble to rebuild our tent had taken some of the fire out of her. Dawn hates losing and, thanks to Mr. Bartholomew, it was clear this would be a long, drawn-out defeat.

On the other side of me stood Darby. Or leaned Darby, actually. She kept slouching over onto my shoulder because she was sleepy. Then again, it could be she was just trying to stay out of Dawn's line of sight. She'd felt so guilty after crashing into our tent and knocking it flat.

"Fine job. Fine job. Fine job," Mr. Bartholomew said to each of the boys. "Now where is this other tent you wanted me to look at?" He glanced all around as if he expected a second tent to hop out from behind a sage bush.

"It's at our campsite, sir," I said. "Follow us."

I gently pushed Darby upright and waited until she seemed awake and steady on her feet. Then I headed toward our camp.

Aunt Jane had gone to help Mrs. Kimbro prep for the lunch rush — making us promise before she went that we wouldn't try any more moneymaking schemes. I was kind of glad she wasn't here to witness our defeat.

"Here it is," I said, gesturing toward our tent — now even more crooked-looking. At least our flag looked good tied to the stick we had staked in the ground nearby. And we'd done our best to clean it. Dawn even swept the grass around it.

I could see the boys' eyes widen. Jay grinned and nudged Robbie and Nelson with his elbows, and Nelson let out a little snort of laughter.

"Wo-ho! I haven't seen one of these old models in years," Mr. Bartholomew said. He walked around it, glancing up and down, just like he did with the boys' tent. Only this time he moved a little faster and hummed a little tune I didn't recognize.

He kept nodding his head and saying things like "Umm hmm" and "Yep." Darby kept nodding, too. At first I thought she was agreeing with whatever he kept *yep*ing to, but soon I realized she was nodding off and then jerking her head back up.

On the other side of me, Dawn let out a long sigh. I knew she was wanting him to hurry up and get it over with.

Mr. Bartholomew completed his circle of the tent, poked his head inside, and chuckled. Then he patted the canvas wall. Unlike the boys' tent, it didn't spring right back into shape. Instead, the whole structure thrummed and wiggled and eventually stood still — looking slightly saggier. "Yes siree, I slept in old shelters like this back when I was in the military," he said. "Oh, this brings back memories. Waking up to see coyotes poking their heads inside, looking for food. Mud everywhere. Yep, those were good times."

Dawn and I exchanged confused looks. I saw the boys do the same.

"All righty, then. I have chosen a winner," Mr. Bartholomew said, standing extra straight as if he were a soldier at attention.

The rest of us glanced around at one another. Finally, I said, "Who's the winner?"

Now Mr. Bartholomew looked baffled. "This one."

"You're kidding me," Jay said.

"What?" Dawn said.

"But . . . but . . ." Nelson stammered. "It's old and ugly. Ours is lots nicer."

"As I recall," Mr. Bartholomew said, "when you approached me early this morning, you wanted me to decide who did the best job assembling a tent — not which tent was the nicest. Well, I happen to know how hard it is to put up one of these doggies." He patted the side of the tent again and it slumped even more. "That new model? It could be set up in a windstorm by a kindergartner."

Jay looked a little shriveled and Nelson's mouth hung open super wide, like a snake about to swallow vermin.

Robbie and I locked eyes. He shrugged and smiled.

"So . . . we won?" I asked, just to make sure I understood. Beside me, Darby kept blinking hard. I wonder if she thought she was dreaming.

"No contest," Mr. Bartholomew said. "This right here was the best effort."

Dawn sashayed forward. A rosy glow had come over her, and her smile gleamed in the sunshine. "Thank you, Mr. Bartholomew, for serving as judge. And for serving our country. We sure do appreciate you sharing your expertise."

"A pleasure," he said with a head bow. "Now if you young folks will excuse me, I want to catch some perch before they stop biting." He strode off down the trail, whistling that same tune I didn't recognize.

"Well, well, well," Dawn said. She slowly strode in front of our tent, running her hand on the canvas in a lazy, carefree kind of way. I still couldn't believe it had won. It looked so slouchy and sad-looking.

"Well, well, well what?" Jay asked.

"Nothing," Dawn said with a sly smile. "Just that . . . *Well*, it looks like we have a legitimate decision by a judge. *Well*, it looks like my team is now officially in the lead. And *well*, what do you know? Your sneaky tactics didn't work."

Jay's eyes narrowed. "What are you saying?"

"Come on! We know that you knew you were renting the last tent. We had to take this old retired one. But we persevered. We pulled together and worked hard, and" — she waved her arms toward our tent in a grand gesture — "managed to build this."

"Yeah!" I added. "Twice!"

"Those are serious allegations," Jay said. "But rather than dignify your assumptions with a defense, I will simply say, congratulations. You might have won this competition, but there's one more contest in this challenge. I propose that our final challenge not be one that requires a judge, but one that is decided by a clear measurement — an indisputable fact."

"Yeah," said Nelson. "You guys just got lucky with judges. That's all."

"Sore loser," Dawn said.

"But what can we do that wouldn't require a judge?" I asked. "What sort of thing would have measurements determine the winner?"

Nelson raised his hand. "I know! Shooting arrows at a target!"

"That's not a camping-related challenge," Jay said.

Nelson scowled.

"I have a proposal," Robbie said. "But it's a little more complicated than the first two challenges."

"Are you worried they can't handle it?" Jay asked with a smirk.

Dawn folded her arms across her chest. "Bring it on."

"Yeah, bring it on!" I echoed. "Right, Darby?"

I looked over and saw Darby teetering beside me. At the sound of her name, she straightened up and blinked her eyes wide. "Yeah," she said.

"Well? What is it, Robbie?" Nelson asked.

Robbie glanced around at us. He kept swallowing and blinking his eyes. I could tell he was nervous about everyone looking at him — Darby gets that way, too, sometimes. It made me feel bad for him.

"Come on, Robbie," Jay said. "You need to officially state it for the record."

"Okay." Robbie cleared his voice. "I propose that our third and final challenge be . . ."

I nodded my head and bounced on my toes, trying to urge him on.

". . . A fishing contest," Robbie finished.

"Yesss!" I shouted raising my fist in the air. I was so proud of him. Then I quickly pulled my arm down. I'd suddenly realized what he said — and I suddenly realized I didn't like it.

Not fishing! Fishing and I went together like . . . well . . . like scrambled eggs and sardines. Fishing takes someone who's not too squeamish to put a worm on a hook — which isn't me. And someone who's able to stand or sit still for long periods of time — which is also not me.

"That'll be cool!" Nelson exclaimed.

"Sounds good to me," Jay said. He turned toward Dawn. "Well? What do you say?"

I figured Dawn understood my predicament and would counter with a different idea. But to my horror, she stuck her chin in the air, held her hand out to Jay, and said, "You're on."

Hi, Alex! How are you? I'm doing

Hi, Alex. This is Darby. Delaney started this, but she's been busy making friends with a donkey and hasn't found the time to finish. I figured I'd go ahead and use the paper.

Camping has been an adventure. Dawn is insisting on us sleeping in a tent to prove we are serious campers. If Delaney or I complain, she reminds us of the conditions Washington's troops faced at Valley Forge.

I guess it's not so bad. You can hear the crickets and the owls. Mainly you can hear Delaney talking in her sleep. Once I woke up in the middle of the night to find Delaney's foot in my face.

I hope you and Lily get to spend some time together during your break. Have you started planning the wedding?

I can't wait until you are my brother. But it feels like you already are.

Love,
Darby

CHAPTER NINETEEN

Pole Results

Dawn

This is all you have?" I asked, lifting one of the three cane fishing poles Mrs. Kimbro had set on the counter in front of us.

Mrs. Kimbro nodded. "That's all I'm able to rent out to folks your age."

"But . . . it's just a stick with a piece of string attached," I pointed out. "There's no reel."

"That's right."

"But . . . my friend Lucas, back home, has a lightweight silvery rod and reel that can catch anything. He says it costs more than his bicycle — and his bicycle is super fancy."

"It sure is," Darby mumbled. She sat farther down the counter, feet dangling from the stool, her sleepy head resting on her arms.

"It's like a bike from the future," Delaney said. She stood behind Darby and was swinging a fishing bucket around. "If the future is fast and gleamy."

"I'm sure it would cost more," Mrs. Kimbro said. "And that's exactly why these are the only poles we rent out to young people." She grinned one of her sympathetic grins at me. "Sorry, sweetheart. I hope you understand."

"Don't worry, Dawnie," Aunt Jane said. She sat at the counter on the other side of me, looking through an old photo album that Mrs. Kimbro had handed her. "You can still catch plenty of fish with a cane pole. I've done it lots of times."

"I guess," I said with a sigh.

"I'll give you pointers," Aunt Jane said. "And you can use my rod and reel and I'll show you how to use it, too."

"Um . . . Aunt Jane? No offense but . . . this is a club thing . . . with the other campground kids. We kind of want to do it on our own. You know. For the experience."

Aunt Jane tilted her head and peered at me closely, like she could see into my brain. "You mean like when you set up the tent by yourselves?"

"Yes. Just like that," I said. "Plus, weren't you going to help Mrs. Kimbro update her website?"

"Oh, honey, that's not pressing at all," Mrs. Kimbro said. "Your Aunt Jane is here to be with you. She and I can catch up later."

"It's fine. Y'all go ahead and visit." I tried to sound casual. "We won't be too long."

"Yeah," Delaney chimed in. "We'll only be fishing for two hours."

I turned and made bug eyes at her to remind her that we didn't want Aunt Jane to know about the contests. "Something like that," I said.

"Well, all right," Aunt Jane said. "At least let me help you with your supplies."

A few minutes later, we set off for the old causeway freshly slathered in sunblock and wearing hats. Darby carried an empty bucket in one hand. In her other, she carried Aunt Jane's cooler, which was full of water bottles, pimento cheese sandwiches, and a plastic container of night crawlers to use as bait. I carried the three cane poles and had Aunt Jane's watch and a tape measure in my shorts pockets.

Delaney, meanwhile, carried a big #3 galvanized washtub that banged against her legs as she walked. The only way we could calm her down about catching fish was to reassure her that we would throw them back after the competition was over. Since the buckets were small and any fish we caught might suffocate after a couple of hours, she convinced Mrs. Kimbro to let us borrow the washtub. All the clanging hurt my head, but at least it scared away Mo. That donkey tended to follow us around like a dog, and I didn't want to run the risk of him coming onto the causeway and maybe scaring away the fish.

Mrs. Kimbro had told us the causeway was an old road from long before the river was dammed up and the lake was made. When a new highway was built several years ago, bypassing their land, the old road was abandoned — yet another reason why fewer people knew about the camp-ground. Apparently, it had always been a good place to fish, but that's all it was now since it's rarely used as a road.

As the causeway came into view, we could see that the boys were already there. They weren't fishing yet, but they'd staked out a spot. Jay was looking over his pole — which, of course, had a shiny reel.

"Dagnabbit. I can't believe we have to use these old poles in a fishing competition. It's like doing a professional bike race with training wheels," I grumbled. "Okay, team. Try not to let them intimidate you."

I wasn't sure Delaney heard me with all her clanging and humming, and I suddenly realized Darby wasn't beside me anymore.

I glanced behind me to see her standing there, staring straight ahead. She was so still, I wondered if she had fallen asleep with her eyes open.

"Darby?" I called out. "Darby, what are you doing?"

She shook her head and blinked her eyes a few times. "Sorry," she said. "It's just so pretty out here."

"It's sparkly," Delaney said, walking in a small noisy circle to take in the surroundings.

It was true. While the causeway itself was just an old stretch of road over a narrow part of the lake, with rocky sides leading down to the water, the area around it was as scenic as a postcard. The campground side was a grassy slope with trees that seemed to be bowing their heads toward the shoreline. The other side was scrubby with chunky limestone hills up above and colorful bursts of wildflowers all over.

"Quit noticing all the beauty!" I said. "We have a competition to win! Pick up the pace, you two!"

Finally, we reached the causeway and approached the boys. Nelson immediately started pointing and laughing.

"Are those your poles?" he asked. As he guffawed, he opened his mouth so wide, I could count his teeth.

Robbie elbowed him. "Stop it," I heard him whisper. "Don't be obnoxious."

"No, it's fine," I said. "Go ahead and laugh. You laughed at our tent, too, remember?"

That seemed to do the trick. Nelson's freckled face went from laughing to scowling in two seconds.

"All right, let's go over the rules," Jay said.

"What's to go over? It's simple," I said. "We agreed to fish for two straight hours and that the team with the most fish wins."

"But remember that only keepers count," Jay continued. "We'll have to identify the fish and make sure they meet the minimum length requirements."

Mrs. Kimbro had given us a color copy of the fish ID guide and a booklet listing the length requirements for each species. I pulled them out of the empty bucket Darby was holding and held it up for them to see. "We will."

"What are you guys going to try to catch?" Nelson asked.

"Fish," Delaney said.

"We're going to catch bass," Nelson said. "And Dad's going to grill them on planks!"

Delaney looked stricken. "That sounds like something a pirate would do."

"So when do we start the two hours?" I asked. "We need a little time to set up."

"Let us know when you're ready," Jay said. "We'll all start fishing at the same time."

We walked along the causeway and set down our stuff in a spot several yards away from the boys. Delaney immediately started heading to the lake with the bucket to fill the tub, but I reminded her that we didn't have any fish yet and that she should wait until our poles were put together.

Delaney and I carefully assembled our poles, putting the pieces together and tying on the bobbers, sinkers, and hooks the way Aunt Jane and Mrs. Kimbro had showed us. Then we built Darby's pole for her since we couldn't be sure she'd stayed awake during the demonstration.

Finally, we had ourselves three finished fishing rods — old-fashioned, but sturdy. I sure hoped they'd do the trick.

"Let's bait our hooks," I said. I took the plastic container of night crawlers out of the cooler and opened it up.

"Aww, they're so cute!" Delaney said.

"Someday those will be your famous last words, Delaney," I said. "Are there any critters you *don't* think are cute?"

Ignoring me, she reached in and pulled out a fat crawler. Next, I put my fingers into the container and grabbed the end of a worm. As I lifted it, it stretched and wriggled like a shoelace come to life. I made a noise like "Yeep" and dropped it back into the container. Then I tried again, but this one twisted around even more than the first, so I went "Yap" and let him go, too.

Meanwhile, Delaney was cooing to her bait. "Hello there, little fella. Hee! You tickle."

"Quit making friends with your worm," I said. "Our opponents are waiting."

Only Delaney wasn't listening. "Look! He's a bracelet." She held out her arm to show the worm wrapped around her wrist.

"Great googly-moogly! Will you hurry up? The boys are waiting so we can start and you're making jewelry out of our supplies!"

Even though the weather was breezy and the temperature was mild, my face felt like it was sizzling. So far, nothing was going the way I wanted it to, and I didn't want the boys to see us acting like a bunch of goof-offs.

I took a deep breath and tried to make the sizzles die down. "I'm sorry," I said.

"I'm sorry, too," she said. "It's just . . . I can't put my worm on a hook. Sorry."

I sighed even deeper. I should have expected this.

"Where's your worm, Dawn?" she asked, glancing down at my hands. "Did you already bait your hook?"

"I . . . um . . . dropped it," I confessed. "It was slippery."

"Are you ready yet?" Jay called out. I looked over and saw all three of them staring at us. Nelson had his hands on his hips.

"Almost!" I called back. That's when I realized Darby still hadn't grabbed her night crawler.

I turned and found her sitting on the causeway, leaning against the cooler with her eyes shut.

"Darby!"

"Sorry," she said, blinking her eyes wide. She scrambled to her feet and glanced around, looking like she'd forgotten where she was.

"You need to bait your hook," I told her, handing over the container of worms.

"And could you please do mine, too?" Delaney asked her. "I just can't."

"Sure," Darby said.

"As long as you're at it," I said, "you might as well do mine. You know. Just to simplify things."

"Sure," Darby said again.

"If there's a way to not prick him, do that," Delaney said. "Like maybe tie him on like a bow?" She turned completely around, shut her eyes, and put her fingers in her ears. "Tell me when you're done," she said loudly and started going "La la la" to the tune of "Yankee Doodle."

When Darby was done, she handed a pole to Delaney. "Don't look down," she said. "Hold on to it and then, when it's time, just lower it into the water."

Darby then handed me a pole and picked up one for herself.

"Are we all set?" I asked.

"All set," Darby and Delaney said together.

"Okay!" I shouted to the boys. "We're ready when you are!"

I heard some murmuring and then Jay called out, "On the count of three. One . . . Two . . . Three!"

All at once we lowered our hooks into the water and they cast their lines. And then . . .

We just stood there.

And stood there.

And stood some more.

Birds called out. The wind rushed through our hair. And we just stayed in place, watching our red-and-white bobbers floating on the water below.

After a while, I sat down and Darby did the same. And we sat there and sat there, holding our poles and waiting.

Of course, it didn't take long for Delaney to get restless. First she started rocking on her feet. Next she began bouncing her pole.

"You shouldn't do that, Delaney. You'll scare the fish and maybe shake off your bait," Darby told her.

"Here. Give me your pole and I'll watch it while you fill the washtub," I suggested.

"Good idea!" she said, bouncing even more. I quickly got to my feet and grabbed her pole, and she went to fetch the bucket.

It was awkward standing there with a long cane pole in each hand. I felt as if I had extra-long arms — like I was a giant praying mantis playing with yo-yos, or an orangutan drummer.

Delaney, meanwhile, kept filling the bucket with lake water and dumping it into the washtub. She was just going down for a third bucketful when her pole jerked in my right hand and her bobber got pulled under the water.

At first I didn't know what to do. I needed to grab the pole with both hands, but I couldn't do that without dropping my pole or getting the two tangled. So I just yelled, "Help!"

Darby saw me struggling, set down her pole, and rushed over. At the same time, Delaney abandoned her mission to get more water and started rushing up the slope shouting, "Fish! Fish! Fish!" Out of the corner of my eye, I could tell the guys were all turned toward us, watching.

Darby grabbed the jerking pole and raised the hook up and out of the water. I thought for sure the fish would be huge, considering how hard it had yanked. But as it flopped on the ground I could see it was only about three inches long — it could fit in my hand.

I heard Nelson start laughing. "Look how tiny!" he exclaimed.

"Dang," I muttered. "Not a keeper."

"No wait!" Delaney said. "It is! Look!" She held up the chart and tapped her index finger on one of the pictures labeled Bluegill. Sure enough, it looked just like our catch. And below it, where the size requirements were listed, it read: "No minimum."

We all three shouted hooray and Delaney and I started singing, "A keeper! A keeper!" in a singsongy way while Darby took it off the hook. She plopped the fish into the tub and we watched it start swimming round and round.

"Aww . . . he's cute," Delaney said.

I heard a noise and saw Robbie jogging over to us. "The guys sent me over to make sure the fish counted as a catch."

I started to fuss and holler and tell him we knew what we were doing — and if it had been Jay or Nelson, I might have. But Robbie always acts so skittish with his big downcast eyes and mumbly voice. It would be like bawling out a baby deer.

Delaney pointed to our catch and then pointed to our size chart. "Yup. See?" she said. "He can be any size he wants to. Says so right here."

Robbie smiled. "Okay. I'll let them know. Sorry to interrupt."

After he headed back to his team, I clapped my hands together. "All right. Back to your stations. Delaney, quit trying to pet that fish. Darby, quit using the cooler as a pillow and wake up. Let's catch us even more fish."

We returned to our poles and Darby put more bait on Delaney's hook while Delaney finished filling the tub with lake water. Then we started the standing-and-waiting part all over again. I felt better, though, now that we were in the lead. According to Aunt Jane's watch, we had an hour and fifteen minutes to go, so hopefully we could stay ahead.

Unfortunately, it didn't last. A few minutes later we heard a commotion and saw the boys jumping up and down. I sent Delaney to check and she came back to say that Jay caught a keeper.

"He said it's a small largemouth bass," she said. "Small largemouth — ha! That's funny. Anyway, it's fifteen and a half inches, so it counts."

This news made my insides feel twisty, so I tried to make myself feel better by remembering that we weren't losing, we were tied.

Only then there came more hullabaloo down the causeway, and the boys started high-fiving one another. Delaney zipped over and back and reported that they'd caught another bass, this time by Robbie. It was almost an inch longer than the first.

"We're losing," I said. I turned toward my pole and stared hard at my bobber, attempting to use willpower to make a fish pull it under. But it just floated there, all peaceful and annoying.

We sat and waited some more, trying to ignore the singsongy voice of Nelson going, "Two fish. Two fish. We got two fish." According to the watch, we had forty minutes to go.

"Your bobber!" Delaney shouted.

"What?" At first I was confused because my bobber still wasn't moving, but then I noticed that Darby's bobber had gone down so far, you could barely see the red. The end of her pole was bent so far, it looked like it might break in two.

But Darby hadn't noticed. Her head had slumped forward and her eyes were shut tight.

"Darby!" I shouted.

Her head jerked up and her eyes opened wide — unfortunately, so did her hands. Her pole zoomed out of her grip and fell. It lay at the top of the embankment and started joggling downhill. Darby kept glancing in all directions, trying to figure out what was going on. By the time she came to her senses, her pole would probably be halfway across the lake.

"I got it!" Delaney yelled. She tossed down her pole, reached way over, and grabbed the end of Darby's pole just as the fish gave it another big tug. "Holy moly! Whatever it is, it's strong!" Her face twisted and turned red as she struggled to pull it up.

I kept standing there, bouncing in place and saying, "Get it, get it, get it!" over and over again. Darby must have finally realized what was happening, because she quickly scrambled to her feet, ran behind Delaney, put her arms around her middle and pulled. Little by little, the line started to come up from the water.

"It's working!" I shouted. "Hang on!" I set down my pole, ran behind Darby, slid my arms around her middle, and started yanking backward. Step by step we went until we finally sped up.

"I see the fish!" Delaney cried. "It's coming out of the water! It's . . . it's huge!"

"What is that?" Darby said. "It looks like a monster!"

I tilted my head to the right and left, but couldn't see anything. At last, with one final tug, we dragged whatever it us up onto the top of the causeway. I let go of Darby and she let go of Delaney and we all stood around the big thing that flopped on the ground in front of us.

"Put him in the tub! Put him in the tub!" Delaney shouted.

"Wait," I said. "We don't know what it is."

It did appear to be a fish, at least — one with a mottled brownish-yellow body, beady eyes, long whiskers, and an enormous mouth.

"According to this, it's a flathead catfish," Darby said, consulting the chart. "Huh. Looks more like an alien than a cat or a fish. If it's eighteen inches, it's a keeper."

I pulled out the tape measure and handed it to Darby, who stood over it and measured from its tail to its pouty-looking jaws. "Almost nineteen inches!"

Again we shouted hooray and did a little victory dance. Then Darby unhooked the beasty fish and, with help from Delaney, heaved him into the washtub. The splash it made as it went in got us all wet.

"What's that?" Suddenly, Robbie was there, peering into the tub.

"A flathead catfish. A keeper!" I said.

"I'm going to name him William Howard Taft — after the president who needed a special bathtub made for him," Delaney said. "And I'm going to name the little fish James Madison."

"You guys name your catches?" Robbie asked.

"She does," I corrected him. "Now go tell your brothers that we're officially tied."

"Still fifteen minutes to go," he said, glancing at his cell phone. "And we've been getting nibbles. Might not be tied for long." He turned and ran back to his pole.

"Come on, come on!" I said, making sweeping motions with my arms. "Pick up your poles and make sure you have bait. We can still win this thing."

Darby re-baited her hook and we all dropped our lines back in the water. This time, I didn't feel bored. Just the opposite. My heart felt like it was jogging and my feet were all jittery. I suddenly understood what it was like to be Delaney.

If the boys didn't catch another fish, we could tie. And if we caught another, we could win. There were only fifteen more minutes — but each minute seemed to last a year.

I focused hard on my bobber, but also kept sneaking glances at my sisters. Darby seemed to be staying awake.

Every time there was a splashing sound from the tub, Delaney would say something like, "Don't worry Taft and Madison. We'll let you go soon." But otherwise, she seemed to be focused on her pole.

I checked the watch. Ten more minutes.

A few seconds later a shout came up from the boys. Nelson was pulling and reeling with all his might.

"Oh no," I muttered. It felt like a big stone had just dropped into my stomach.

Then another cry went up — but not a happy sounding one. I glanced over and saw the end of Nelson's line swinging free.

"Why'd you yank up so hard?" Jay was saying. "You pulled it right out of its mouth."

And suddenly I could breathe again. I checked the watch. Six minutes. Then five. Then four . . .

Anytime my bobber made the slightest movement, I gave a little tug. But there was never anything there.

Three minutes. Two minutes. One . . .

"Time!" Robbie called out.

"Time!" I called out a second later.

It was over. Another tie.

"At least we didn't lose," Darby said. "And we did our best."

The boys walked over carrying their stringer with the two bass hanging off it. "We want to measure your fish and make sure they're keepers," Jay said.

"Yeah?" I said. "Well, we want to measure yours, too."

Suddenly, Delaney let out an anguished sounding cry. She stood over by the washtub, her arms waving around all herky-jerky. "Oh no! No no no no no!"

"It's okay, Delaney," I said. "We'll let the fish go after they check the length."

Delaney spun around to face us. Her eyes were big and saggy and her mouth was quivering. "It's awful!" she said. "A terrible tragedy!"

"What is?" I asked.

"We only have one fish."

"What the heck are you talking about?"

"William Howard Taft ate James Madison."

CHAPTER TWENTY

Unknown Threat

Darby

Dawn had been so pouty about our loss, even our afternoon game of Frisbee with Aunt Jane wouldn't cheer her up. For dinner we had franks and beans — one of our favorite meals — but she was sulky through that, too. Delaney and I tried to remind her that even though we'd lost the fishing competition, we tied in the overall challenge. Both teams were just as good. But that didn't seem to help.

I was just glad it was over.

After tent judging, fishing, and Frisbee — and no sleep the night before — I was so tired, my head was having problems staying up. It kept drooping forward or lolling back. When we ate dinner in the camper, I could barely concentrate on the food. I kept looking over at the bunk where Dawn and I had slept just two nights earlier. It looked like the most comfortable spot in the world — like a cottony cloud. I wanted so badly to crawl up onto it and close my eyes.

Aunt Jane caught me yawning. "Y'all take out your trash and get ready for bed. It's been a big day."

"You all right, Dawn?" I asked as we headed outside. Even the Moon Pies we'd eaten for our Daily Chocolate didn't bring a smile to her face.

"I'm fine. Just thinking," Dawn said, keeping her gaze fixed on the empty wrapper in her hand. She had that look on her face. The one where her eyebrows push against each other over her nose, and her mouth moves around like she's chewing something. Sometimes she taps her finger against her chin or makes small grunting noises.

"What are you thinking about?" Delaney asked.

"I'm trying to come up with a good tiebreaker challenge."

"But . . . why?" I asked, leaning in closer to try to catch her eye. "Can't we just leave it as a tie?"

Dawn glared at me. "No! We can't be 'just as good.' We have to be better."

"But why?" Delaney asked.

"We just do! Because we are! Don't you get it?" She crumpled up her wrapper and stomped over to the trash can.

Delaney looked over at me and shrugged.

"Um . . . Dawn? I think we're all worn out," I said. "Maybe we should sleep in the camper tonight and get some good rest."

Dawn whirled around and scowled at us — ten times worse than her previous angry face. "No. No way. That would be taking a big step backward. It would be like admitting defeat."

"But it was a tie." I felt like one of those toys that said one of three things when you yanked a string on its back. In my case it would be *Why*, *But we didn't lose*, and *It was a tie*.

Dawn let out a loud sigh. "We're still going to win this. Somehow we're going to show those boys that we're the best." She turned and headed back into the camper.

Delaney gave me another shrug. "I'm not inclined to argue with her. Are you?"

I shook my head no. As it was, I was so zonked, it probably didn't matter where I slept.

Finally, we finished cleanup and it was time for bed. I didn't even bother to change clothes. I just staggered out to the tent, crawled onto my sleeping bag, and laid my head on my pillow. My thoughts got all fluttery and I fell asleep right away. But the next thing I knew, Dawn was poking me awake again.

"There's a wild animal out there," she said. "It sounds like it's ready to attack."

"What?" I sat up and saw Delaney and Dawn peering out the back window of the tent.

"Just listen," Dawn said.

"It's probably Aunt Jane snoring," I said and started to lie back down.

"No. It's not," Delaney said. "It's coming from the wrong direction."

I paused to listen. Sure enough, the weird growly noises were coming from the nearby bushes.

"What if it's a swamp monster?" Delaney said.

"There's no such thing, Delaney," Dawn said. "It's probably Bigfoot."

"I'm sure it's nothing to worry about. Just one of those feral hogs like Old Mr. Maroney keeps finding on his land back home," I said. But even as I said that, I didn't totally believe it. My sleepiness was still there in my body, but now my brain was focused on the noises. "We should go investigate."

There was a long pause.

"Um, no, thanks," Delaney said. "I'd rather stay here."

"Me, too," Dawn said. "It's not that I'm afraid; I just think I could do a better job of handling the situation from here. If you get eaten someone's got to tell Aunt Jane."

I was used to this sort of thing. Delaney is always willing to do the running around if we need to deliver a message or get something from the store. Dawn has no problem talking on the phone or asking questions of authority figures — like the stern lady who works in the school office. And my job has always been to check out potential dangers. Usually it's a spider or the ghost that lives in our mom's bathroom.

"Fine," I said. "I'll go see what it is. If anything goes wrong I'll holler."

I ducked out of the tent and tiptoed toward the noises, watching where I stepped so I didn't crack a twig or crunch leaves or make any sound that might startle whatever it was. I really did think it was a javelina or raccoon — but I kind of hoped it was something less common. Like a chupacabra. Or maybe a yeti.

The idea of facing things like that scares most people, but I feel that if such creatures exist, they are probably misunderstood rather than dangerous. And maybe I could help them and become their friend. Maybe I could broker peace with the species on behalf of all humans!

Of course, if the noises were being made by something dangerous, I figured I could at least shout a warning to my sisters and all the rest of the campers before I got carried off to a hidden lair. Just to be safe, I picked up a fairly hefty-looking stick off the ground and carried it with me.

The strange sounds were coming from the Neutral Zone, and were getting both louder and clearer as I crept closer. At times there came a squeal — at other times, a low grunt. I had decided it was definitely a feral hog when suddenly I heard it go, "No fair!"

For just a second, I thought, "A talking feral hog!" But as I stepped into the clearing, looking down to spot the critter, I spied a pair of white sneakers tramping around the brush — and those sneakers were attached to Nelson. He was stomping around with clenched fists, muttering and sniffling. Occasionally he'd wipe his cheeks angrily or pick up a pebble and throw it. I felt bad for him, but I wasn't sure what to do.

As I watched, he suddenly let out a growling sound and kicked the tree next to him.

"Hey, Nelson! Whoa! Take it easy," I called out, stepping forward and dropping my stick.

Nelson yelped and jumped backward. Once he realized who I was he scowled and kicked at a twig on the ground between us. "Leave me alone! I don't even like you guys, so just go away!"

I probably should have been mad to hear him say that, but I wasn't. I could tell that this was the kind of angry that comes from feeling bad inside. I wondered if his family knew he was out here.

"Nope," I said, and leaned against one of the trees. "I think I'll stay."

"Go away!"

I shook my head. "You know I don't have to. This is our time to have the Neutral Zone, so technically you are on our campsite. Besides, you're making such a racket, we can't sleep."

He paused and peered past me. "How many of you are out here?"

"Just me. When I heard noises, I got worried, so I came to investigate. I'm still worried. You seem upset."

"Well, I'm not upset."

"Well, you sure look upset to me."

"What do you know? You're a girl."

I put my hands on my hips. "What does that have to do with it?"

"You don't know what it's like to be a little brother."

He had a point. "Maybe not. But I do know what it's like to feel bad about things. Want to tell me why you're crying?"

"I'm not crying!" Nelson folded his arms across his chest and stomped around in a small circle.

"Okay. Sorry. But you should know that it's all right if you are."

"I'm not crying!" Nelson shouted again. Even as he glared at me, the faint light from the moon showed shiny wet lines on his cheeks. "Boys aren't supposed to cry!"

"Well, that's just silly. Where'd you get that idea?"

"Colby Bixby says that boys who cry are wussies."

"Colby Bixby? Is he a doctor or a philosopher?"

"No. He's a kid in my class," Nelson said, making a face. "He's just a bully guy."

"Seems like a lousy role model. I wouldn't trust his advice."

"Yeah," Nelson conceded. Then he frowned at me. "But you aren't a doctor or anything, either."

I nodded. "Fair enough. What do your brothers and your dad say about crying?"

"I never asked them," he said. "Besides, I don't care what they think. They took my bow and arrow away."

"Why?"

"Jay and Robbie told Dad that I wasn't being careful."

"Were you?"

He shrugged and looked down at the ground. "I was just

trying to shoot it and run at the same time. I didn't mean to crack the window. It was an accident."

"I have accidents all the time. And I get punished sometimes, too," I said. "I think it helps to let the tears come out. It helps me."

Nelson didn't saying anything. He just kept dragging his feet over the ground. But I could tell he was listening, so I kept on talking.

"Lots of people want to be alone when they cry, and that works, too. One of my sisters is that way. Sometimes she even crawls under her bed so no one will see her."

Nelson stopped in his tracks and looked at me. "Really?"

"Yep. But at least she lets it out. So maybe you could just . . . try it? See if you need to cry and then let it happen."

"Like an experiment?"

"Like an experiment."

He seemed to consider this. "And you'll leave me alone and you won't tell anyone? Not even your sisters?"

"Cross my heart," I said, drawing the intersecting lines on my chest with my finger.

Nelson still looked worried.

"Tell you what," I said. "If I do tell anyone, I'll . . . I'll eat a worm."

"For real?"

I nodded solemnly. "I will. We still have some bait leftover. If I tell, I'll swallow a whole night crawler."

"Whoa." His eyes grew big and he seemed to calm down a little. "All right. Thanks."

I straightened and started brushing the leaves and dirt off my shorts.

Just as I turned to walk away, I heard him say, "It gets lonely out here," he said. "I miss my mom and my friends. Sometimes my brothers treat me like a little kid."

"Sometimes I get treated that way, too," I said. "It stinks."

"Yeah. And I was mad that I didn't catch that fish. We could have won. I mean . . . we still won, but only because one of your fish ate the other one."

"We almost didn't catch that big fish — because of me. I actually fell asleep out there."

For the first time, Nelson smiled. "It is kind of boring. I guess I could see why."

He still seemed a little glum, but a lot calmer about it. It made me feel good to talk to him this way — like a big sister, sort of. Delaney was born only seven minutes after me, so she didn't really count as a younger sibling.

"Well, anyway, if you could keep it down, I'd sure appreciate it," I said. "I really need to sleep."

"I will," he said.

I turned and started heading back to camp. "Bye, Nelson. I hope you feel better."

"Bye . . . whichever girl you are."

CHAPTER TWENTY-ONE

Eminent Domain

Delaney

The next morning, we slept late. We know this because Aunt Jane left us a note on the table inside the camper. It read:

> Good morning, girls! I thought I'd let you sleep in. There's cereal for breakfast, so dig in. I went to see if Tammy needs any help at HQ. Please come by after you've eaten and we'll go do something fun.
>
> Aunt Jane

"I feel awful," Darby said. "We haven't done enough to cheer up Aunt Jane."

"Yeah. We were so focused on the Great Camping

Challenge, we haven't spent that much time with her the past couple of days," I said.

"But the competition is important," Dawn said. "We can't stop now. We still have to do something to show those boys we're the best. For the sake of our family honor. For decent people everywhere!"

"Aunt Jane is decent. She's got family honor," I said.

"And she's probably lonely because we've been doing our own thing." Darby plopped down on the bunk. She looked so guilty, it made my stomach hurt. Or maybe that was also because I needed breakfast.

"Well, what are we supposed to do?" Dawn said. "The horses are gone. The canoes leak."

"We're not allowed to ride the donkey," I added.

"We don't have to do special campground stuff," Darby said. "We could just swim or play cards."

"That's all fine and dandy, but I still think Aunt Jane is just flat bored," Dawn said. "She's used to Boston, where big things happen. Fireworks and festivals where people pile into the streets and . . ." She broke off and stared at the wall. Her eyes went big and round and her mouth also made an O shape.

At first I thought maybe she saw a tarantula or a scorpion, but when I followed her gaze, I didn't see anything.

"Dawn? You okay?" I asked.

"That's it," she mumbled. "I'm brilliant."

"Um . . . How are you brilliant this time?" Darby asked. The slow, gentle way she said her words made me wonder if she was afraid to ask.

Dawn started pacing about the way she does when she's making plans — only she had to go in a tiny circle since the trailer was so narrow. "I know how to cheer up Aunt Jane in a way that isn't humdrum or boring. A way that might even liven up this lackluster campground." She paused and stood in her Wonder Woman pose — hands on her hips, legs apart, and chin raised high. "The three of us are going to put on a parade!"

While the parade was kind of silly, it really wasn't a bad idea. Maybe if we hadn't been such show-offs, the day wouldn't have taken such a sorry turn. Our mistake was letting Dawn be in the lead.

We forgot she was still trying to prove something to those boys.

We finished planning the parade as we ate breakfast. When were done, we dressed in clothes that were red, white, or blue, applied sunscreen, and pulled up our flag pole. Then off we went, single file, singing "When the Saints Go Marching In" and stepping to the rhythm.

Dawn was in front carrying our flag pole. Darby marched in the middle holding a cardboard sign in front of her that read HAPPY LAKE LEWIS DAY! I took up the rear and managed to coax Mo to follow along behind us — mainly by putting lots of carrots and apple pieces in my pockets.

The day was cloudy and windy, and the flag flapped wildly in the breeze. In a unanimous vote, we'd decided to take the road instead of the narrow trails, so that we wouldn't have to poke through the brambles and risk ripping our flag. We marched down the gravel drive of our site and onto the asphalt lane that wove through the campground. Only instead of turning left, toward Camp HQ, Dawn turned to the right.

"Where are you going?" Darby shouted.

"Quick detour," Dawn said. "Let's stop for just a second."

She reached back and flipped over the sign Darby was holding. Somehow that morning, without our noticing, she'd written CAMPSITE 19 RULES! BEST TEAM IN LAKE LEWIS! in big letters on the other side.

"Okay, now we're ready," she said, taking her place in the front again. We restarted the song and Dawn led us down the drive for Campsite 18.

The boys were sitting at their picnic table. Nelson had been stretched out on his stomach across one bench, but he sat up and frowned at us as we approached. Robbie waved and I waved back. Jay, meanwhile, just watched us the entire time. His face was blank, so I couldn't tell how he felt.

There was TV noise coming from inside the RV, but no one peeked out — at least not that I could tell.

After we made a circle of their camp, we went out the way we came. "Great going, troops!" Dawn called out, reaching back to flip back Darby's sign. "That'll show them what kind of team we are." She was all smiles.

Darby and I exchanged a shrug.

Next, we headed down the road, toward HQ, marching and singing and luring Mo with a carrot. Mr. Bartholomew was headed the same way with his fishing pole. As we caught up to him, he saluted at us . . . and then fell into step beside me! It made me laugh to see his bony knees bouncing high as he marched. Occasionally, coins would fall out of the pockets of his shorts.

Soon we came upon some more campers, including John Michael, the boy who had paid us to ride Mo. He took one look at us and ran into his family's tent. I worried he was upset with us, but then he came back out wearing a red rain poncho and carrying a recorder — just like the ones we play in music at school. He also started marching with us and blowing on the recorder at the same time. The tune didn't exactly match our song, or any song that I knew, but it still added to the celebration.

It was amazing. As we passed more campers, a few others joined in. Some older men like Mr. Bartholomew, a few more younger kids like John Michael, and a couple of older ladies — one of whom had a loud singing voice, almost like an opera singer. Some clapped as they sang, someone whistled, and a couple of people shook wads of keys like maracas. Lots more folks waved and smiled as we went past.

As we entered the big grassy area by HQ, I spotted Aunt

Jane and Mrs. Kimbro sitting on the patio. They pointed at us and started laughing and clapping. I watched as they disappeared into the building, and came back out carrying a couple of things. Mrs. Kimbro jogged up next to Dawn and kept lifting a spatula like a baton to the music. Aunt Jane fell into step beside Darby and started banging together two pot lids like cymbals. It was so much fun I was bouncing with glee and kept getting out of step to the beat.

Unfortunately, the lid banging scared off Mo, and soon our voices were wearing out. So after one more loop around HQ, Dawn held us in place until the chorus ended. Then we stopped.

The people around us clapped and cheered for a while before going their separate ways. Mr. Bartholomew gave us one more salute and continued his trek to the old causeway, and John Michael turned and smiled at me. "I want to work here, too, someday," he said, and ran off toward a group of kids, blowing on his recorder.

Mrs. Kimbro and Aunt Jane were heading back to the table on the patio. We ran after them. As we caught up to them, I noticed Aunt Jane was smiling big and laughing. It was so great to see.

"Did you like that?" Darby asked her.

"I sure did," she said. "What's the special occasion?"

"We're celebrating our freedom and our patriotism and . . . um . . ." Dawn paused.

"And our right to have a parade!" I added.

"Lake Lewis Day," Mrs. Kimbro said, reading Darby's sign. "I like that. We should make that official."

Dawn grinned so big at that I thought her face would never recover.

"We want to keep celebrating with a swim and a picnic at the beach," I said. "Would you guys like to join us?"

"Another great idea," Aunt Jane said.

"I'm honored, but I'm afraid I have to stick around here and work," Mrs. Kimbro said.

"If you don't mind, I'll stay a few minutes longer to help Tammy with some work we started," Aunt Jane said. A map and some old photographs lay on the table in front of them. I figured they were probably reliving fond memories again. "How about I meet you down there? I'll bring sandwiches and some candy bars for our Daily Chocolate."

We all cheered at that. Then we saluted them good-bye and the three of us headed for the exit.

"Didn't Aunt Jane look happy?" Darby said as we stepped outside.

"She sure did!" I said, bouncing as I walked. "They both did!"

"Told you it was a great idea," Dawn said.

As we skipped down the grassy slope toward the swimming beach trail, I spotted Mo hunkered under a tree and ran over to him.

"Aww . . . Now he looks bored," I said. "He's sad the parade is over."

"I think he looks worn-out," Dawn said.

I was just reaching into my pocket for a carrot stick for Mo, when Darby elbowed me in the side. "Look," she said, nodding toward something behind me. I spun around and saw Jay, Robbie, and Nelson heading toward us in a line.

"No way!" Dawn said.

"They're having a parade!" I pointed out — although I didn't need to.

Sure enough, the three of them were marching in time. Their flag was hanging behind them, off the back end of a long stick. Jay was the head of the line, of course, and the main thing I noticed as they came closer was the flinty-eyed look of determination on his face. His jaw was set and he refused to meet our gazes, staring just beyond us instead.

"Lousy copycats!" Dawn exclaimed as they passed within a few feet of us.

As they went past, they quickened their step, and then went faster and faster until they were running toward the trees.

"Weird," Darby said.

"Yeah. Our parade was way more festive," I said.

"Y'all *should* run, you plagiarizers!" Dawn shouted after them, shaking our own flag stick. "That's not even proper marching technique!" The look of victory she'd been wearing before was gone. Now she was scowling and muttering things like "low-life stunt" and "cheap imitation."

We decided to continue our trek to the beach and wait for Aunt Jane. I tried to get Mo to come with us, but he seemed determined to stay where he was. Maybe he was hoping there'd be more parades.

As soon as the lake came into view, we ran into Nelson. He was standing right where the walking path opened up onto the pebbly beach, looking as if he'd been waiting for us.

"You can't be here," Nelson said, his mouth in a lopsided smirk. "We've already claimed this space."

"Claimed it?" Dawn repeated.

He nodded and pointed toward the shoreline where their flag had been planted in the middle of the beach. Jay stood beside it all puffed up and proud-looking, while Robbie sat beside him looking bored.

"You can't do that!" I said as I pushed past Nelson. Dawn and Darby followed.

Nelson ran over to stand beside Jay. "Y'all are just mad that we got here first," he said, raising his chin.

"We're mad because it's wrong," Dawn said.

"It's not wrong," Jay said. "It's manifest destiny. The universe wants us here."

"And just how do you know that?" Dawn asked.

Jay smiled. "Because we thought of it, and you didn't."

Dawn jammed down our flag pole, shoving the stick into the pebbly dirt with a *chunk* sound. Her arms went rigid beside her and her eyes narrowed into thin slits. I wouldn't have been surprised to see tiny explosions under her feet, lifting her off the ground and sending her soaring like a missile — right for Jay's head.

I instinctively took a few steps to the side.

There came a loud rumbling, and I shielded my eyes, waiting for the blast. Only . . . it never came. The next thing I knew, I felt a drop of wet on my forehead. Then more and more.

That's when I realized that the booming sounds hadn't come from Dawn, but the sky. In an instant, it was raining hard. More thunder sounded, and the rain hitting the lake made a noisy *shhhh* sound.

Dawn didn't move. She stood so straight and unyielding, we probably could have hung a flag off her, too. She just kept glowering at the boys — who were now abandoning the beach and running toward us.

Nelson passed us first, heading back up the trail in the direction of the campsites. Robbie followed, grinning apologetically as he went by. Then came Jay, carrying their flag.

"You can use the beach now," he said to Dawn. "Just remember that it's ours."

Dawn just kept standing there, staring menacingly at the lake, pretending to ignore him.

After they passed, I grabbed our flag pole and gave it a big yank. "Come on," I said, pulling it out of the dirt. "We should get back, too." But Dawn didn't budge.

"Forget about those guys," Darby said, picking up one of Dawn's stiff arms and pulling it. "The competition's over."

Dawn nodded. "You're right. This isn't a competition anymore," she muttered.

I felt a little rush of relief.

She turned her head to meet our worried gazes, and the look in her eyes made me gulp. "This is war."

CHAPTER TWENTY-TWO

Rain of Terror

Dawn

This place hates me," I mumbled.

"Again, Dawn?" Delaney asked. "I thought you decided you wanted to stay."

"I do want to stay," I said, sounding whinier that I'd meant to. "I was just remarking."

My squishy creek-water shoes had finally dried out and now they were wet again. But then again, so were everyone else's. Maybe the campground hated all of us. Maybe it was anti-Brewster.

Aunt Jane had come back from HQ to check on us. She invited us into the trailer, but I insisted that we were fine eating lunch in our tent. I felt like we needed to regroup and plan our countermove in private.

Beside me, Darby lay stretched out like a starfish, trying to take a nap — although I wasn't sure how anyone could rest. The rain sounded like sixty-five people with drumsticks pounding the roof of our tent. Meanwhile, Delaney kept wriggling around, accidentally jostling us.

"Mo!" Delaney was on her knees, shouting out the back window of the tent. "Mo! Here, Mo!" She made a loud whistle that hurt my ears.

"Ding-dang it, Delaney! Why do you keep on calling that donkey like a dog?"

"Well, how would you call a donkey?"

"I wouldn't!"

"I just worry about him being out there in the rain."

"He's been living out here since we were in diapers, Delaney. He doesn't need you to look after him. Besides, we're supposed to be plotting our next strike against those scoundrels."

"But I thought we were done battling the boys," Darby said.

"How many times do I have to say this? We're *not* done!" I said. "No way are they getting the last move."

I noticed Darby and Delaney exchanging looks, but I didn't care.

On the other side of Darby lay our soggy flag, which we'd taken down off its pole. The marker colors had run a little, but the design was still clear. Each time my eyes passed over it, it reminded me of the competition and my gut felt all bunched up. I'd been so sure we would win. How could I ever hope to be president if I couldn't even win a camping standoff?

The incident at the lake rattled me a little. Okay, maybe a lot — especially right after our accidental loss of the fishing contest. I'm used to always being a step ahead of everyone. And this was the first time I'd met somebody just as high-reaching as I was, not counting my sisters.

Aunt Jane had always said we were exceptional. Only . . . here was some boy at the very same campground, at the very next campsite, who also plans to be president someday. So maybe I wasn't as special as I thought.

In the beginning, it made me mad that Jay thought he was smarter than me. But here's a secret: Now I was worried that maybe he actually was — and that scared the tarnation out of me.

Even as I sat there trying to plot our next step, I was all shaky on the inside. I worried that I'd lost my mojo. Or that I never had it in the first place and just fooled myself for almost twelve years. Everything I'd been working toward was now in question.

There had to be some way we could defeat them — or at least get Jay as riled up as he got me.

"What if we made lots of flags and put them everywhere else in the campground except for their campsite and the lake?" I suggested. "We could beat them at their own game!"

"But . . . it's raining." Delaney pointed out the window. As if I couldn't see, hear, smell, and feel it.

"Also, it took a long time to create our flag," Darby said. "I'm not sure we have the time or supplies to make more."

"What if we infiltrated the boys' camp and stole their food?" I asked.

Delaney's mouth fell open. "That's unethical."

"Or what if we snuck over there and sewed their tent shut while they're inside it?"

"That's dangerous *and* unethical," Darby said.

"You two could be more supportive of my ideas, even if they are lousy," I said. "It's impossible to come up with one of my brilliant plans under these conditions."

Even as I said it, I knew that was a lame excuse. If a president were in a bunker somewhere having to come up with strategies to help the nation, she couldn't give up and blame it on bombs exploding outside or meteorites falling all around.

"Besides," I added in a grumbly voice. "Those boys started it. They're the ones who've been playing dirty."

Just then, a horrible honking sound came from the other side of the canvas wall. I nearly jumped to my feet and ran off, bringing the tent with me.

"It's Mo!" Delaney shouted. "He's here! He came to see us!"

The girl was so excited, she was practically turning cartwheels.

"All right, all right. Hyper down. That's all we need is to have to set up this tent a third time."

"I want to give him a little snack as a reward," Delaney said.

"Don't make him sick," Darby warned.

"I won't. It'll just be a little one." She looked all around the tent. "Where are the chips?"

"Over there in the corner," I said, pointing.

As Delaney lifted the bag, she let out a cry of surprise. "Huh? Why are they dripping?"

Darby and I crawled over to see for ourselves.

"Oh no!" Darby said. "There's water coming into the tent!"

Sure enough, there was a big puddle in the front left corner of the tent with a few chips floating in it. It had already soaked the edge of Darby's sleeping bag and was quickly spreading.

"There's no way we can stay out here," Delaney said. "We have to move back in with Aunt Jane before we're all underwater."

"No!" I shouted.

Darby placed her hand on my arm. "Dawn, what are we trying to prove?"

"That we're the best at governing!"

"But . . . look at us." Delaney gestured around the wet, mildew-stained tent. "How is staying out here going to do that?"

"We've gone along with your plans all this time, but it's time to stop," Darby said as she continued to pat my arm. "There's competitiveness and there's foolhardiness."

"But . . . but . . ." I stammered. But I knew they were right. Our lousy award-winning tent was falling apart. We had to go back to the camper.

It seemed like a sign — a warning that no matter what we tried, we couldn't prevail. None of my plans were working, and of my teammates, two were naysayers to all my ideas and one was a wet donkey.

I hated giving in. It felt like Jay was getting the last move. But for the first time in my life, I didn't know what to do. Maybe I wasn't a great leader after all.

Dear Lucas,

Sorry if this letter is smudged. It got rained on. Also, the stain in the corner is a bit of tuna. Plus, Darby accidentally lay down on the paper, so it got rumpled.

Have you ever been camping? If you do go, here are some things you probably want to bring:

· Your fancy fishing pole

· A comfy bed

· A safety net

· Surveillance equipment for spying on suspicious characters

Sincerely,
Dawn

CHAPTER TWENTY-THREE

Great Depression

Darby

It was raining the next day, too, but my wish had come true and I was back to sleeping on the soft snuggly bunk in the trailer.

After we ate cereal and did some Mad Libs together, Aunt Jane went to HQ to help Mrs. Kimbro and promised she'd return for lunch. Dawn, Delaney, and I played six straight games of Spite and Malice — most of which I won — and then we were officially sick of cards. So we all spread out to various parts of the trailer to do our own thing.

Normally, I don't mind being cooped up during bad weather. I even love it. It's like an automatic lazy day. A time to stay indoors and lie around reading and dreaming. There's something about doing nothing with your body that lets your imagination go leaping and playing about.

But Delaney still just leaps about the regular way — rain or shine.

That girl was driving me bonkers. She was running from one window to the other yelling out at Mo, making excuses to open the door so she could sneak him snacks, and singing songs substituting "Mo" for part of the lyrics.

Like . . . "Rain, Rain, Mo Away!"

Or . . . "Mo, Mo on the Range!"

Or . . . "Happy Mo Day to You!"

Usually, Dawn would stop all that commotion with her fussing. Only Dawn didn't seem to be herself. She was like a soda with no more fizz. She'd barely paid attention to her cards during the games, and was now slouched in the corner of the bunk looking sullen. Even Aunt Jane's promise that morning to bring back cupcakes only brought out a lackluster *whoop* from Dawn.

"What's with you?" Delaney had remarked. "You had more vigor and verve when you were asleep."

Dawn just mumbled something about the rain being a big downer, but I wondered if there was more to it than that. She had so little spirit. I wished I could drain some of Delaney's energy and volume and pour it into Dawn.

I reached my breaking point when Delaney started singing the Star Wars theme using only "Mo" as lyrics ("*Mo MO! Mo-mo-mo MO! Mo*"). As she sang, she hung upside down on the padded bench, drumming out rhythms on the underside of the table.

While Delaney banged and warbled, I crawled over to

where Dawn sat slumped in the corner of our bunk and sat beside her.

"We need to have an emergency meeting," I said.

"Good luck," she said. "Delaney seems . . . busy."

"No. I mean, we need to call a meeting *about* Delaney. Just you and me."

She looked right at me and raised her eyebrows. "I'm listening."

"If the rain doesn't stop soon and I end up in this camper with Delaney for much longer, I'm going to have a fit."

"You?" Dawn seemed somewhat impressed. "You hardly ever lose your cool."

"That's why I'm coming to you. I've hit my limit," I said with a sigh. "I have no idea how you are dealing with this ruckus."

"I reached my limit the first day into this accursed trip. You know that." She reached down to scratch her left leg. The ant stings were now just tiny red dots, but they probably still itched.

"Yeah. Sorry," I said.

She lifted her shoulders in an *oh, well* type of gesture. "Nothing I can do. And there's nothing we can do about Delaney, either. We just have to accept that we're stuck in a dungeon of torment and despair. At least we get cupcakes later."

"Maybe," I said. "But I think I have an idea."

Dawn looked doubtful. Either she was too deep in her wallowing to imagine a way out or she didn't believe me capable of coming up with a plan.

"What is it?" she asked.

I glanced over at Delaney. She was still hanging upside down, but was now singing "The Star Spangled Banner" with all "Mo" lyrics. Then I scooted as close to Dawn as I could and whispered, "The van."

"What about it?"

"Let's convince Delaney that she should go spend a few hours in there. We'll say it's like having her own room. That way she can be closer to Mo and get as loud as she wants. Then you and I can stay here and enjoy the peace and quiet."

"Wow. That really is a good idea."

"Thanks." I puffed up proudly. Dawn is stingy with praise, which makes it even more powerful when it's used.

I waited for Dawn to do what she does best — to plot out the best way to put our scheme in motion. Instead she crawled to the edge of the bunk, reached for her shoes, and started slipping them on her feet.

"What are you doing?" I asked.

"I'm calling dibs on the van."

"Wait . . . *What?* But we were going to get Delaney to go out there. We agreed!"

"No, we didn't. We just talked about it. And I've just now reserved the van for myself."

"But why?"

She paused in her activity to shoot me an incredulous look. "To escape this pain and torture. Why do you think?"

"That's not fair!"

"You should have claimed it first if you wanted it."

"But with my plan, if Delaney goes out there, everyone benefits. If you go out there, only you do!" I scooted off the bunk and stood in front of her. "You aren't being democratic. You're being . . . a lousy opportunist!"

"Oh yeah? Well next time you call a secret meeting about Delaney, you should follow proper procedure. We never actually voted on a plan of action, so no rules were broken."

Dawn must have said this during one of those rare, brief periods when Delaney was quiet because suddenly she was right there beside me.

"You called a secret meeting about me?" Delaney said to me. "How could you? I thought we were partners after you and I had the meeting about Dawn."

"About *me*?!" Dawn cried, leaping to her feet.

"Don't act so surprised," I said, putting my hands on my hips. "You're the one who's always going on and on about democracy and official procedure, but then you went and entered us in that competition without even asking us first!"

"I can't believe this!" Dawn waved her arms and shouted up at the ceiling. "You guys had a meeting behind my back!"

"She called it." I pointed at Delaney.

"So? I learned it from you." Delaney pointed at Dawn. "You called one about Darby."

"What?" It felt like cold needles were jabbing my stomach. "You guys met without me?"

"We had to," Dawn shouted. "You were endangering us all with your daredevil wilderness antics. This is camping, not a jungle safari!"

"Backstabbers!"

"Double-crossers!"

"Turncoats!"

A loud whistle pierced the air, making us all freeze. I spun about and saw Aunt Jane standing in the open doorway of the trailer, holding a plastic container of cupcakes.

"You girls are louder than grandpa's Sunday tie," she said. "Now . . . Who's going to tell me what's going on here?"

CHAPTER TWENTY-FOUR

Crossfire

Delaney

We were a sorrowful sight — and probably a sorrowful sound, too. I lay crying on one bunk, Darby was across the trailer crying and hiccupping on the other bunk, and Dawn was under the table pretending she wasn't upset, even though she was.

Mo wasn't even outside anymore. Apparently, we'd scared him off with our loud bickering.

"I am not having a good time," I said. It was probably obvious considering I was sobbing into a wadded-up blanket, but I felt like it needed to be stated.

"This is the worst vacation ever," Dawn said.

"We aren't — *hic!* — united in fun," Darby said in a shuddery voice. "We aren't even united."

Meanwhile, Aunt Jane sat on the padded bench, listening quietly and occasionally passing us all tissues.

We were all hurt that the other two had undercover meetings where we'd each been excluded and then talked about. We felt it was unfair, unkind — and unconstitutional. After all, full representation is a necessary part of democracy, and until recently we'd always followed proper technique.

But in addition to being mad at my sisters, I was mad at myself. I don't mean to be such a live wire — that's just how I am. Only I sometimes forget that my activity and chatter can get on other people's nerves. I need to keep that in mind more.

I guess, by the same token, Darby can't help that she's such a risk taker and Dawn can't help being so pigheaded. No matter how maddening it can be, they are who they are. Normally, we're defending one another from people who don't understand us. So it hurt extra bad that we were turning on each other just for being ourselves.

Once the wailing had died down to whimpers, Aunt Jane said, "Know what I think? You gals are suffering from an acute case of cabin fever."

"But we're in a trailer," I pointed out.

"All right then. Trailer fever," Aunt Jane said. "You've been cooped up too long together and it's natural you'd get on one another's nerves."

"They hate me," Dawn said.

"No, they hate me," Darby said.

"Even Mo doesn't want to be seen with me anymore," I said.

"Now, now," Aunt Jane said. She hopped up to hand us all another round of tissues and then sat back down at the table. "No one hates anyone or anything. And I blame myself for spending all that time with Tammy these past few days."

"It's not — *hic!* — your fault," Darby said.

"Maybe not entirely. But the point is, it's natural you three would be going a little stir-crazy," Aunt Jane said. "I went through this exact sort of thing myself with your mom when we were girls."

I lifted my head to look at Aunt Jane. At the same time, Darby rolled over to look at her, and Dawn leaned sideways from her spot under the table to take a peek.

"*Hic!* How so?" Darby asked.

Aunt Jane laughed quietly. "Oh, Annie and I . . . We used to drive each other batty. I thought she was so smug and bossy . . ."

Darby and I both snuck a look at Dawn. We couldn't help it.

"And she thought I was irresponsible and into disgusting things," Aunt Jane went on.

Dawn and I snuck a look at Darby.

"And neither of us could keep still or quiet for longer than two minutes," she added.

Dawn and Darby turned their gazes toward me.

Aunt Jane sat back against the bench cushion and took a quick peek out the window behind her. "Rainy days were always the worst," she said. "Actually any day when we were trapped together, just the two of us. We'd always end up doing things on purpose to make each other mad."

"Like what?" Dawn asked.

"Oh, you know. The usual. Hiding the other person's shoes. Pouring a little Tabasco sauce into the other's oatmeal bowl. Putting geckos into the other's sleeping bag."

"That's awful!" Darby exclaimed. But she was chuckling a little. So was I. Even Dawn had a small grin on her face.

"And I used to say terrible things." Aunt Jane shook her head and her mouth made twisty motions — just like Dawn does when she's upset. "I'd holler that I couldn't wait to move out and we'd finally be apart. I'd tell her that once I graduated, I'd move far away from her and never ever come back."

I sucked in my breath. I couldn't imagine Aunt Jane saying such a thing.

"And you know what?" Aunt Jane asked.

"What?" Dawn said, climbing up onto the padded bench beside her.

"I did end up moving far away from home. And do you know what happened?"

"What?" I asked, taking a seat on the bench next to Dawn.

"I missed my sister something awful," Aunt Jane said, her voice cracking a bit. "I realized she was the best friend I ever had — and ever would have — even if she was sometimes smug and bossy."

Darby shot off her bunk and sat down on the other side of Aunt Jane, leaning against her.

"Truth is," Aunt Jane went on, "I still miss Annie lots and lots when I'm not near her. And I miss you three girls, too."

Now we were all hugging her. Tears were running down my face again, but they were different kinds of tears. The kind that happen when you love someone so much, it hurts.

"And — *hic!* — do you miss Lily?" Darby asked.

"Of course Lily."

"And Dad?" Dawn asked.

"I miss that goofball, too."

"And Quincy?" I asked.

"That rascal pup?" She laughed. "Why, yes. Even him."

"We miss you, too, Aunt Jane," Darby said. "Whenever you aren't with us."

"It's true," I agreed.

"All the time," Dawn said.

"Aww . . ." Aunt Jane threw her arms around us and pulled us a few inches closer. "You girls are the best. And the point I'm making with all this is that it's okay to need a break from family. But never forget how lucky you are to have one another."

That was when our gazes moved from Aunt Jane to each other. I'm not sure who said it first, maybe Darby. Maybe Dawn. It might even have been me. But suddenly we were all saying, "Sorry!"

"We can do better," Darby said.

"We can survive this," Dawn said.

"If we managed to peacefully coexist in the womb," I said, "we should be able to share a trailer."

We got up from the bench and did a group hug — one of those big, squeezy hugs where you shut your eyes and hold on tight. And after a while, the feel of your arms on the other people — and their arms on you — sort of blends, until it seems like you've been fused together.

United.

CHAPTER TWENTY-FIVE

Internal Affairs

Dawn

Finally, it stopped raining.

When I opened my eyes the next morning, everything seemed brighter and the birds sounded like they were catching up on gossip after a long break. I unzipped the flap on the window beside my bunk in order to check the weather.

The first thing I saw was a big furry nose.

"Mo!"

He hee-hawed at me and shook his head, so I figured he was begging for some food. I was about to call to Delaney and tell her to sneak him a carrot stick when her face appeared next to him. I should have known she'd already be up.

"You and Darby need to get dressed and come on outside," she said. "Aunt Jane is treating us to breakfast at HQ. They have hot chocolate and everything. And she said I could give Mo another apple." Her fast talking blended in with the bird twitters.

Normally, I find Delaney's loud chatter annoying in the morning, but I was still feeling guilty after our big argument the day before.

I had already known, inside my brain, that my sisters and I wouldn't always be together. But it wasn't until Aunt Jane talked about how hard it was to be across the country from Mom that I actually *felt* it. The thought of being far away from Darby and Delaney for long stretches of time gave me a jittery sensation — cold and lonely and slightly panicked. Like when I'm playing Marco in Marco Polo and everyone seems too unreachable.

I shook Darby awake and we headed outside. Mo had already wandered off by the time we got out there, and Aunt Jane was putting some supplies back into the van. Apparently, she'd been hard at work clearing our site of twigs and other debris that fell during the rain, and she got rid of as much standing water as she could, so that mosquitos wouldn't breed in it. She also took down our tent. I felt a little twinge of regret as I saw all the pieces laid out to dry in the sun — but also a whole lot of relief.

I took a moment to admire Aunt Jane for being so diligent and even-tempered. Maybe when I became president, I should offer her a spot in my cabinet, as well as make her an advisor.

"You gals ready for some grub?" she asked. "I figured we'd eat out today instead of cooking it here. But first thing's first." She took off her work gloves and set them on the picnic table. "Can't forget the guidelines."

Aunt Jane headed over to the grassy area and did a perfect cartwheel. Darby, Delaney, and I applauded and then, one by one, did our own.

"Now off we go," Aunt Jane said. As she started down the path to HQ, the rest of us looked at each other.

"After you," I said sweeping my arm toward the path.

"Why, thank you," Darby said. "Watch out for this mud puddle."

"Thank you very much," Delaney said. "Let me hold this branch out of the way."

We were like that the entire way, saying "please" and "thank you" and warning each other of potential threats. I complimented Delaney on getting up early and Darby complimented her on her great relationship with Mo. Delaney complimented Darby for being such a quiet sleeper and I complimented her on getting dressed so quickly. Then Darby complimented me on my posture, and Delaney complimented me on never confusing *capital* (with an A) with *capitol* (with an O), since she always gets those confused.

We hadn't had a fight among all three of us in a long time. When it happens, it's scary and we end up on our best behavior afterward. I wondered if Aunt Jane's reminder that we wouldn't always be living under the same roof — or tent — had unnerved the two of them as much as it did me.

"Good morning!" Mrs. Kimbro sang out when she saw us. She stood behind the food counter, waving at us with a dish towel.

"Good morning, Mrs. Kimbro!" we chorused.

"Hello, young ladies!" came another voice. We turned to see Mr. Bartholomew smiling at us. "I recommend the hash browns," he said in a low voice. Then he put on his fishing hat, tipped it to us, and headed out the screen door.

Mrs. Kimbro told us that Mr. Bartholomew came every spring for two weeks. "It's our regulars like Ned who keep us afloat," she said to Aunt Jane, spreading bacon in a pan. "But they can't come forever. And we've already had one family pack up and leave, on top of three other cancellations because of the rain."

Aunt Jane started sharing stories of when business was bad at her tavern in Boston and how once, when her savings ran out, she sold some belongings to make extra money — including a basketball autographed by all the former Houston Comets.

It felt a little like we were eavesdropping, even though we weren't trying to. So when our plates were ready, I suggested we take them out to the patio area.

The big covered deck was empty except for us, so we snagged the table with the best view. The lake sparkled in the sunlight, and it looked like someone had swept every wisp of cloud from the sky. I took a deep breath of fresh air and slowly let it out.

Somehow I'd been erased of bad stuff — just like our campsite and the wild blue yonder above us. Those angry thoughts and feelings I'd had seemed to have washed away.

After we settled into our seats and got past all the "after yous" and "please pass the salts" and "thank you very muches," I leaned forward and said, "Troops, I think maybe we should have a meeting. An official one."

We waited as Darby fetched paper and pencil so she could take minutes.

"First things first," I said once she was back. "Let's have a motion to ban all secret meetings forever more."

Delaney raised her hand. "I move that from here on out, all meetings must involve all three of us."

"I second it," Darby said.

I banged my fist on the table three times. "Motion passes. Good job. And . . . I'm sorry."

"I'm sorry, too."

"I'm sorry three."

"Also" — I paused to take a breath and swallow a lump in my throat — "I want you to know that I never want to move far away and that I like being around you guys — even when you drive me nuts."

"Me too."

"Me three."

We smiled at each other — and our smiles were sad and proud at the same time.

"But you know," Darby added, "we won't be far apart — at least not for long. Because we'll all end up in Washington D.C. working hard for this great country."

"Maybe we could even share a house," Delaney suggested, hopping in her seat.

"We could share the White House!" I said.

Everyone agreed that would be the best plan.

We sat and ate our food in peaceful silence for a while. I felt much better after our talk, but I still had a nagging sensation at my center. Even though things were settled among me and my sisters, I knew we'd run into those boys at some point — and that they'd probably do something that would make me lose my temper all over again. I just wasn't sure what to do about that.

I must have been lost in my own thoughts because I didn't realize that Delaney had left the table. Suddenly, I heard a *pssst!* sound and glanced up to see Delaney way over at the edge of the deck, motioning us with her hand. "Come here," she whispered.

Most people get attention by raising their voices. For Delaney, the opposite is most effective. Delaney sitting still and whispering is a rare, remarkable phenomenon — almost unimaginable. Like hearing Darth Vader giggle. You can't help but pay heed.

Darby and I tiptoed over and hunkered down beside her. Then we stared out into the brush in the direction her finger was pointing.

In the grassy area near the tree line were three deer. They stood there, each facing a different direction, eating shoots of weeds and grass. As they foraged, they kept a sharp eye out around them, occasionally pausing to stare closely in a particular direction. They were so beautiful — dainty but also regal looking. I wasn't sure how long we crouched there, watching them. After a while, a notion sprang up in my mind — like a tiny grass shoot. Only instead of getting munched on by a deer, this one grew and spread out until it was a solid plan.

"Troops," I said, and my word seemed to break them out of the spell of the deer. "There's one more thing I need to talk with you about before we adjourn the meeting."

We headed back to the table and sat down. Darby and Delaney looked at me expectantly.

"I need to confess some things to you. And if you all don't mind, I'd prefer that Darby leave this off the record." I blew out my breath and gazed down at the tabletop. "Since we've arrived I've been a big stress ball. I worried about getting attacked by wild critters, that the trailer would tip over, that a snake would make its home inside my shoe — you name it. I just felt kind of . . . powerless. But when we started up the Great Camping Challenge — that helped me. It made me focus on other things and stopped my imagination from running hog wild."

"We noticed," Delaney said.

Darby nodded.

"I thought we'd win the competition easy — but it proved harder than I thought. And I guess I got . . . carried away."

"We noticed that, too," Delaney said.

Darby patted my arm.

"But you know what? I don't think I need it anymore. Some things are more important." I reached out and put a hand on their shoulders. "If it's all the same to you, what do you say we put an end to this rivalry once and for all?"

CHAPTER TWENTY-SIX

Clean Air Act

Darby

The trek to Campsite 18 was soggy. The ground squished and water dripped on us from the overhead branches. I didn't mind, though. At one point I found deer tracks in the mud, and I wondered if they were the same deer we'd seen earlier. I also liked how the rocks were all glisten-y after the rain, and I put a couple of extra-pretty ones in my pocket.

I took a deep breath and smiled. The expression "clear the air" really did fit — in the sense that the rain had washed away all the dust, but also because Dawn, Delaney, and I had gotten rid of the bad feelings that had been building up. The day was fresh and clean and new, and so were we.

We actually didn't have to hike all the way to the campsite because the boys were sitting in the Neutral Zone. They had dragged out three folding lawn chairs and planted their flag in the open spot where we come through. We had to inch around it to step into the clearing.

I thought Dawn would yell at them about it, but she didn't. However, she did push the flag pole as she went past so that it ended up lopsided.

We stood facing them. Dawn was in front, with Delaney and me flanking each side.

"If you came to claim the area, you're too late," Nelson said. "We got it. And not just for mornings, either."

"You guys can plant your flag on every rock in this place for all I care," Dawn said.

Nelson and Robbie exchanged surprised looks.

"Have you come to brainstorm a tiebreaker challenge?" Jay asked. "We still need to find a winner."

Dawn assumed her best posture and cleared her throat. "Just the opposite. We've come in peace to tell you that we are ceasing all further rivalry. It's been interesting, but now it's time to put all competitiveness behind us."

"So you're admitting defeat," Jay said.

"All right!" Nelson whooped, lifting his arms in the air. "We win!"

Dawn put her hands on her hips. "It's a tie, not a defeat."

"But you just said you are pulling out of the game."

"The game is over."

"Not if we do a tiebreaker."

Dawn smiled her you're-getting-on-my-nerves-but-I'm-not-going-to-show-it smile. "Look, all this battling is pointless. The goal of our camping trip was to spend quality time with our aunt, not ramble about battling strange boys."

"Hey!" Nelson cried. "We aren't strange."

"But you agreed to the challenge," Jay said.

"So?"

"So the object of the game was to figure out who was best. We haven't done that yet, so we still need a tiebreaker," Jay said. "If you don't do it, it's pretty much the same as giving up."

Dawn sighed through her nose. "All I'm saying is, we have better things to do with our time. And we have more important folks to spend our time with. No offense. I'm sure you understand." She smiled again, but I could tell she was forcing herself to. I was amazed that she hadn't started yelling yet, and I was proud of her for keeping her composure.

"All right," Jay said, getting to his feet. "You're saying it's a lack of time, not a lack of determination."

"Yes. That's it!" Dawn clapped her hands together. "Finally, you get it."

"So if that's the case, why don't we do one more contest between us?" Jay paced in front of Dawn, keeping his eyes on her. "A game that would decide the victors once and for all. It shouldn't take long. You'll still have plenty of time to spend with your aunt."

"What kind of contest?" Delaney asked.

Jay stopped walking and stood in front of us, looking smug. "Capture the Flag."

"Ha!" Dawn scoffed. "Forget it. That has nothing to do with good governing."

"Sure it does. You'd have to come up with a plan and work together, right?"

Dawn opened her mouth as if she wanted to say something, and then shut it. She seemed to be mulling over his argument.

"Also, we leave Lake Lewis tomorrow. It's now or never," Jay said. "So are you in? Or are you conceding defeat?" He sat back down on his chair and turned an ear toward Dawn, to show he was listening for her answer.

Dawn made a bleating sound. It sort of looked like she was slowly turning inside out. Her eyes narrowed, her lips were bunched up, and her cheeks were all sucked in. It was probably hurting her not to accept to the challenge. She'd promised us she would put this behind her, but I knew how competitive she was.

Delaney, meanwhile, was dealing with the stress the way she normally does — through movement. Her knees bounced and her hands waggled and her eyes kept zooming around. It was like Dawn was pulling inward, and Delaney was ready to burst apart.

"If you don't respond, we'll interpret it as you forfeiting the tiebreaker challenge."

"Which means we win," Nelson said.

It bugged me how Jay leaned back in his lawn chair as if it were a throne, his bent arms on the metal rests, hands pressed together at the fingers. Didn't he realize how hard it was for Dawn to admit she'd been wrong to enter the competition in the first place? Did he have to hold losing over her head, too?

"Come on. Y'all have to answer us," Nelson said from his chair. "We don't have all day."

"You have five seconds," Jay said to Dawn. "Four . . ."

Wavy lines appeared on Dawn's forehead, and she sucked her lips into her mouth.

"Three . . ."

Delaney started jogging in place.

"Two . . ."

"We'll do it!"

The sentence rang out and sort of hung in the clean air for a few seconds. Suddenly, everyone was staring at me. It took a moment to realize that I had yelled out the words.

Whoops. I guess things weren't as clear as I thought.

CHAPTER TWENTY-SEVEN

Preamble

Delaney

As we walked back to our campsite, Darby just kept shaking her head and saying, "I can't believe I got us into this. I don't know what came over me."

"I'd say some fire got into you," Dawn said.

"I'd say some of Dawn got into you," I said.

"I understand why you accepted Jay's challenge in the first place, Dawn," Darby said. "It's hard to not take the bait."

Dawn gave a solemn nod. "It's like he puts you in a catch-22," she said. "He's kind of an evil mastermind."

"An archenemy," I said.

"A true antagonist," Darby said.

We stepped off the trail onto our campsite. Up ahead we could see our pop-up camper. An Aunt Jane–shaped figure passed by the window.

"You know we're going to have to tell Aunt Jane about

Capture the Flag," Dawn said. "She's going to wonder where we're headed off to."

"Let's just tell it to her straight," Darby said. "Hopefully this thing will be over soon."

"And victory will clearly be ours!" Dawn exclaimed, raising her fist in the air.

When we reached our trailer, Dawn blocked the door and turned to face us.

"Now, no dilly-dallying," she whispered. "We agreed to meet the boys at the Neutral Zone in twenty minutes, so I want us to be there in fifteen. We'll just explain everything to Aunt Jane, grab what we need, and go."

"I hung the flag out to dry this morning," I said. "I'll go get it."

While Dawn and Darby stepped into the trailer, I jogged around to the other side where I'd spread out the flag on a big branch. As I squinted into the trees searching for it, something rustled in the bushes nearby. I figured it was Mo coming to greet me.

"Hey there, old pal," I said.

"Hey."

Huh? I whirled around and saw Robbie coming forward, out of the brush. He seemed extra stooped and shy, and kept glancing over his shoulders.

"The other guys don't know I'm here," he said. "They think I'm scouting flag-hiding locations."

"Are we supposed to be doing that?"

He shrugged. "Maybe. I don't know. It was an excuse to follow you guys." He paused and let out a long sigh. "I just wanted to say . . . I don't like that this challenge thing is still going on."

"Me either," I said.

Robbie glanced all around and took a step forward, out of the brush. "I'm going to tell you a secret."

"Um . . . okay," I said.

"I want you guys to win."

My eyes popped wide. "You do?"

Robbie nodded. "Jay is always doing stuff like this. He thinks the way to prove we're a solid team is to win everything. But I don't want us to be just a team. I want us to feel like . . . a family."

I just stood there with my popped-out eyes, trying to sort out his words. I hadn't really ever thought of what family feels like. I guess it was a little like being on a team, only different — like Robbie said. Deeper and better, but also scarier sometimes. Like the difference between an Olympic swimming pool and the ocean.

Then I laughed because I started thinking about our trip to the coast last spring break and how Dawn opened a bag of corn chips and got surrounded by a zillion seagulls.

But also I laughed because I felt nervous talking with Robbie in secret — not that it was terrible or anything. It wasn't.

I clamped my hand over my mouth. "Sorry," I said, lifting my fingers so he could hear me. "My sisters say I laugh too much, and at all the wrong times."

Robbie smiled, and I noticed that it made his eyes less droopy and that dimples, like tiny quote marks, appeared on his cheeks. "That's okay," he said. "I like it when you laugh. I told you."

A fizzy sensation whooshed over me, as if my insides had gone all bubbly. I giggled a little more and kicked the toe of my sneaker into the ground.

"Anyway," he said, "I just wanted to say I was rooting for you guys and that I hope we lose."

My smile fell away. "Hang on a sec," I said. "Are you telling me you're going to sabotage your team's efforts?"

"No!" Robbie's eyes went saggy again. "That would be dishonorable. I'm going to do my best, but I'm still kind of hoping you'll beat us. It's . . . complicated. I don't know why I'm telling you all this. I just wanted you to understand that I don't see you as our rivals — even though you kind of are." He shook his head as if he were trying to erase everything in it. "Anyway . . . I'll see you soon at the Neutral Zone. Good luck."

"Bye." I watched him turn back into the bushes and trudge toward his campsite. Then I grabbed our flag and headed toward our trailer.

When I stepped inside, Dawn and Darby were sitting across the table from Aunt Jane.

"Wait. Tell me again. You're doing what?" Aunt Jane asked.

"Capture the Flag," Dawn said. "With those camper kids we met."

As we applied sunblock, we reviewed the newly-agreed-upon rules of the game in a way that wouldn't worry Aunt Jane. (Actually, Darby and Dawn explained. I was still feeling a little fuzzy-brained after running into Robbie.)

Because we were in a campground, we'd decided to change up the usual way of playing so that we'd have more room and not bother other people in their campsites. The flags, we had decided, would be placed up high in a tree or some other elevated location, so that they could be seen. Once spotted, the opponents had to retrieve it and take it back to the Neutral Zone before the others. Whichever team got there first would win.

"Hmm. Sounds like it could take a while. And you know that more rain could be headed this way." Aunt Jane shook her head. "I don't know, girls. I think maybe you should put it off until tomorrow."

"But they're leaving tomorrow," I said.

"This is our only chance," Darby said.

"It probably won't take that long anyway," Dawn said. "Just a couple of hours."

"Well . . . I have to say I'm glad you're making friends," Aunt Jane said.

Dawn made coughing noises.

"And you girls have done a good job being cautious and following rules on this trip," Aunt Jane went on. She glanced out the window again and heaved a sigh. "Tell you what. If you see lightning or it starts raining really hard, you come right back here. Deal?"

"Deal!" we said together.

"Well, we probably should get moving," Dawn said, getting to her feet.

"Yep." I craned my head to glance at Aunt Jane's watch. "It's almost time to meet the others."

"All right. Be careful, and have fun," Aunt Jane said.

We told her we would and promised to have one of our epic Frisbee games when we returned. Then Dawn tossed our flag in a backpack and slung it over her shoulder, and the three of us stepped out into the muggy midday air.

"Poor Aunt Jane," Darby said as we headed toward the Neutral Zone. "I can't believe we're still doing this silly competition. All because of me."

"Don't worry," I said. "She still seems happy. And we can always do another parade for her."

"Besides, you've never been able to turn down a dare, Darby," Dawn said. "I know when we got here, I nagged you about being reckless, but this is one rash decision of yours I agree with."

Something went *ping!* inside me — like a tiny Christmas light coming on.

"Wait . . ." I held out my hands in a halting gesture. "I

think I have an idea." I waited for my idea to come into focus inside my mind. Yep. It was a good one all right. I was so excited, I started hopping on my toes.

"What? What's the big idea, Delaney?" Dawn asked, sounding impatient.

I smiled proudly. "I know where we should hide our flag!"

"Where?"

"Where this whole mess started," I said, bouncing on each word. "Darby, how high up that old rope swing do you think you can climb?"

CHAPTER TWENTY-EIGHT

Searches and Seizure

Dawn

Players get ready . . ."

To make sure no one peeked we took turns hiding our flags. I sat with the boys while Darby and Delaney hid ours on the swing by the creek. Then Jay sat with us while Nelson and Robbie hid theirs. Everything was in place. Now we were just waiting for the game to officially begin.

"On your mark . . ."

We all stood in a line next to Jay, who was had assumed the duty of starter. I glanced down to make sure my shoelaces were tied so that I didn't trip. Robbie was standing next to me, and as I bent over, I noticed something about his shoes. Something that made me go "*Hmmm . . .*"

"Get set . . ."

I checked Nelson's shoes, too, and they looked similar. A series of thoughts clicked into place.

"*Go!*"

Darby, Delaney, and I raced out of the Neutral Zone. Delaney quickly zoomed out in front, followed by Darby and me. Everything was nutso, with people running this way and that.

"Guys, wait!" I called out. "Darby and Delaney, hold up!"

Darby turned and circled back to me. Delaney came to a skidding halt and wavered in place a bit before reversing direction.

"We need to talk about where we're going," I said.

"Do we even have a plan?" Darby asked.

Delaney shrugged. "I was just going to run around looking up."

I pulled them into a huddle. "You guys, I know where they hid their flag. We have to go across the creek to the bluffs."

There came a loud gasping sound beside me. I turned and saw Nelson crouching behind a nearby bush.

Dagnabbit! I should have anticipated that they'd use spies.

Nelson saw that I noticed him and ran off into the thicket — probably to find his brothers.

"See? That means I'm right," I said to Darby and Delaney. "Come on. Let's hurry."

We ran down to the creek that divided the low-lying campgrounds from the bluffs and headed for the little bridge we'd spied on our first day there. I winced as our sneakers clattered over the wooden boards. The boys didn't need a spy now to let them know where we were going.

When we got to the other side, we paused and looked up over the choppy-looking hills.

"That's a lot of trees," Darby remarked.

"Maybe we should spread out?" Delaney said. "We could cover more ground that way."

I tapped my finger against my chin. She was right, but that would also mean going against Aunt Jane's guidelines. "I don't know . . ."

The wind was picking up and I realized the temperature had fallen a few degrees. Clouds like steel wool were grouping together on the horizon.

"Nope," I said. "We're sticking together."

"Let's zigzag up the slope," Darby said. "That will cover more ground and we won't get confused as to where we've already looked."

"Good idea."

By the time we reached the top of the hill, we still hadn't found their flag. To the right of us was the edge of the property with a thick barbed wire fence cordoning it off. No way could they have gone in there without getting grated like cheese. To the left was a line of craggy limestone bluffs that stretched in the direction of the lake.

"This way," I shouted, waving toward the bluffs.

It wasn't possible to zigzag here. It required more of a loop-the-loop because of the big boulders and clusters of trees. So we spread out, but stayed within shouting distance.

The sun was completely blocked out by clouds now. I heard the rain before I felt it. The ground beside me seemed to be making popping noises. Looking down, I saw big drops striking the chalky soil. Water started dripping down the branches onto me.

Right at that moment, I heard Delaney shouting. "I found it! I found it! I found it!"

"*Shhh!*" I said, running toward Delaney's voice.

Sure enough, there was the boys' flag, flapping in the wind near the top of a scrub oak. Delaney was doing a little victory dance beneath it.

"Now we need to get it down," I said. From my spot right below the tree, the flag seemed ridiculously high.

Darby easily clambered up the tree and grabbed it. For a change, I was glad she was so surefooted and gutsy. She was slow and deliberate — careful to find the right footholds and handholds. It was clear she knew what she was doing.

As she climbed down I could hear a familiar clattering sound in the distance. The boys were racing across the bridge.

"Hurry!" Delaney whisper-shouted up to her.

"But continue being careful!" I added.

Delaney was running around in little circles with her arms up, saying, "They're coming. They're coming. They're coming." I expected her to get airborne at any second.

With a little jump, Darby hit the ground and held up the flag triumphantly.

"Don't celebrate yet. We still need to get it to the Neutral Zone," I said.

"But I heard them. They're headed this way," Delaney said. "What if they try to stop us?"

"Let me see the flag," I said. Darby tossed it to me and I quickly stuffed it into our backpack. "Now here's the plan. We head back to the other side of this ridge. Keep looking up at the trees as if you're searching for something. And try not to look victorious! We'll make them think they arrived just in time."

"But maybe they already won," Darby said.

Delaney shook her head. "If they had found our flag, wouldn't they be back in the Neutral Zone whooping and hollering in victory?"

She was right. "Come on. Let's put our plan into motion," I said as I started jogging away. "Time to look frustrated and fretful."

The boys found us at the top of the hill we'd zigzagged, staring anxiously up at the trees. Even Darby, who could probably win a World's Worst Liar Competition, managed to have a defeated look on her face. Jay peered closely at us and seemed relieved.

"Did you guys get the flag?" Nelson asked.

I lifted my chin. "Maybe we did and maybe we didn't."

"Do you have ours?" Delaney asked.

Jay copied me. "Maybe we do and maybe we don't."

Then we all just stood there, like another clump of trees, letting the rain fall on us.

After a while, Nelson leaned toward Jay and whispered, "I'm gonna go check —"

"Stop," Jay interrupted, lifting his hand like traffic cop. "We're all staying right here."

Nelson looked baffled. "But . . ."

"Dude, think," Robbie whispered to Nelson. "He doesn't want you to show them what direction it's in."

"Oh. Yeah, we're staying right here." Nelson folded his arms across his chest and scowled at us.

Meanwhile, the rain was coming down harder and harder. My hair and clothes were soaked and it was even dripping from my eyelashes, making it tough to see. At home we like to play in the sprinklers, and it was a little bit like that — except it was cold and scary and there probably wasn't ice cream waiting for us nearby.

"We need to be getting back," I said. "Our aunt doesn't want us out in bad weather."

Jay cocked his head. "So you're quitting?"

"Don't start that again!" Darby shouted.

"Um, guys? I don't think any of us can get back right now." Robbie was crouched down next to a tree, peering over the edge of the ridge. "Look at the creek."

We all knelt down to see for ourselves. Sure enough, the creek, the same one that had been murky green and completely still when we arrived, was now muddy brown and roiling — as if it were angry. It had swollen in size and over-taken the banks. Anything not fixed deep into the earth, like bushes, plants, and mounds of dirt and gravel, were getting pushed into the churning water and sent swirling downstream.

A flash flood. We'd learned all about them in school, but I'd never actually seen one in person. I knew we'd have about the same chance as a leaf against all that rushing water.

"Oh no! The bridge!" Delaney pointed downstream at the bridge — the one the boys had just crossed minutes earlier. The noisy wooden boards were now a few inches underwater and the whole structure seemed to be shuddering under the force of the current.

Now we were stuck on this side of the campground.

CHAPTER TWENTY-NINE

Cliffhanger

Darby

Huddling on a narrow rocky ledge is worse than being stuck in a pop-up trailer. It was about the size of a bus stop — if a bus stop had a big rocky roof over it that prevented you from standing up straight.

Dawn, Delaney, and I sat together on one end, rubbing our arms to try and stay warm. The ground was rough beneath us, so we were all squirmy. Delaney especially. Plus, I kept getting the hiccups.

At least we weren't out in the rain, though. The storm was now right on top of us and sounded like the end of the world. Water was falling from the limestone ledge above in a thin, yellow-colored curtain. And every minute or so, there'd be a flash and a loud thunderclap that sounded like bombs bursting in air.

Big storms are always scary, but being outside during one is extra scary.

"I — *hic!* — I wish I was at home," I said. I meant for it to sound more like a factual statement, but my voice came out all wobbly.

"There, there," Dawn said, patting my arm. "No sense getting in a tizzy." I knew she was trying to make me feel better, but her voice was quaky, too.

"I can't help it," I said. "I miss Mom."

Delaney nodded. "I miss my rabbit."

"I miss the microwave," Dawn said.

Both Delaney and I gave her puzzled looks.

"I mean it. I've had it with pioneer living. Camping is for the birds."

While we sat there all dreary and hiccup-y, the boys were clustered at the other end of the ledge. They were talking in hushed voices and kept looking at us. Jay and Nelson were frowning, but Robbie seemed especially agitated. He kept pumping his arms and shaking his head. If there'd been more room, he probably would have been pacing around. Occasionally we'd hear him say, "No!"

"How long are we going to have to be here?" Delaney said, squirming as if she couldn't get comfortable.

"I don't know," Dawn said.

"I bet Aunt Jane is worried sick about us," I said. "This is — *hic!* — the worst thing we've ever done. Ever." My voice cracked again, and this time a couple of tears leaked out of my eyes. Probably no one could tell, though. That's a benefit to being soaking wet.

"Hey, guys."

I turned around and saw Robbie standing all hunched over. His eyes were saggy and sad-looking.

"I want to quit my team and join yours," he said.

"Wow. A defector," Dawn said. "We sure didn't see that coming."

"What's wrong?" Delaney asked.

Robbie scowled. "I've been falsely accused of wrongdoing, and I don't want to be in a group that doesn't believe me."

"You're overreacting," Jay called out from his end of the ledge.

"You're the one who's blaming me for no reason," Robbie called back over his shoulder. "It's ridiculous."

"Aiding the enemy is not ridiculous. It's very serious," Nelson said.

"Aiding the enemy?" Dawn repeated. "You mean *us*?"

Robbie rolled his eyes. "They think I told you guys where our flag was."

"They came right to this area. They figured it out way too fast," Jay said. "It can't be coincidence, so just admit you helped them."

"I heard her. Right after Jay said 'Ready, set, go' that girl said she knew that the flag was in the bluffs." Nelson pointed at Dawn. "Plus, Robbie's been complaining about this game since it started, and he's always acting friendly with them."

Robbie just stood there, all stooped and sullen. I felt bad for him. Sounded like they had rebellion in their ranks, too.

It made me glad that we'd had our big fight in the privacy of our pop-up trailer.

I scooted as far as I could until I was up against the wall. Then I patted the ground beside me. "Here," I said to Robbie. "Have a seat. *Hic!* You're welcome to join us."

"Thanks," he said with a small smile.

"Robbie's learning how to cook from his dad," Delaney said.

I thought about my mess-up with the fishy eggs, and our Mother's Day Pancake-Making Fiasco. "We need a good cook in our ranks," I said.

"Look at him. I bet he planned to join them all along," Nelson said to Jay.

"Ahem." Dawn stood — or got to the highest crouching position she could get in — and faced the boys at the other end of the ledge. "Do you want to know how I knew where your flag was?"

Nelson jabbed Jay in the ribs with his elbow. "A confession!" he hissed.

Jay narrowed his eyes at Dawn. "Yes."

"I noticed y'all's shoes," Dawn said. "Robbie and Nelson had yellow streaks of limestone all over their shoes. Like we have now." We all glanced at our feet and saw she was right. "There's not a lot of limestone on the other side. I figured they had to have crossed to the bluffs."

"Oh." Nelson looked like he was trying to make himself smaller.

Jay closed his eyes and hung his head. "Right," he said with a long sigh. "I should have thought of that."

"Now do you believe me?" Robbie said.

Jay nodded in a forlorn kind of way.

"Good," Robbie said. "But I'm still staying over here."

Dawn sat back down and clapped him on the back. "I hereby move to officially add Robbie . . . um . . . What's your last name?"

"Moyers," he said.

"I hereby add Robbie Moyers to our United in Fun troop," Dawn said. "Everyone in favor say 'aye.'"

"Aye!" said Delaney and I. Thunder boomed, and it sounded like a big bass drum accenting the moment.

Then we all shook hands and welcomed him.

I took a quick peek at Jay and Nelson sitting silently at the other end of the ledge. I felt sorry for them, losing their teammate like that. But I felt sorry for Robbie, too, getting accused of something he didn't do. And I felt sorry for Aunt Jane and the others who were back at camp worrying about us. And I was sorry for all of us being stuck out in the storm. Sorry seemed to be everywhere.

But I didn't want to feel sorry or scared. I wanted to be United in Fun, so I proposed that we play a game to pass the time and take our mind off the storm. Delaney lobbied for Spite and Malice, but we didn't have our cards with us and Robbie didn't have any, either. Robbie suggested I Spy, but that was a big bust. Most everything was gray or limestone-colored.

"I know a good game, and it doesn't take cards or any-thing," I said.

Robbie grinned. "Great. What is it?"

"Have you ever played Presidential Trivia?"

CHAPTER THIRTY

Outcome

Delaney

Robbie liked Presidential Trivia!

He guessed a lot of them and didn't pout when he was wrong. He knew all the presidents who had been assassinated, who was on U.S. currency, and that Martin Van Buren was the first president who was born a U.S. citizen. And he guessed half of the presidents who had first served as vice president.

When we told him that President John Tyler had had fifteen children, Robbie said, "Whoa." And when we told him that Harry S. Truman had been a haberdasher, he laughed and said, "Wow." He also agreed that *haberdasher* is a terrific word. I think he's going to like being United in Fun with us.

Once I overheard Jay mumble the answer to one of our trivia questions. I wondered if he wished he could play.

It was so hard to sit on that cramped ledge, but luckily, Presidential Trivia got my mind off of my pent-up jitters. We got so caught up in it I almost forgot where we were and what was going on around us.

We had just stumped Robbie on which president wrote crossword puzzle clues for the *New York Times* — Bill Clinton — when Jay called out, "Hey! The storm's dying down."

I glanced up and, sure enough, there wasn't a sheet of water running down the roof of our little nook anymore. I could look out and see the sky, which was now the color of a dolphin instead of almost black.

I got up and stuck my hand out beyond the ledge. "Yep. I only feel a little bit of rain," I said. "And the wind isn't so strong."

As I scanned the horizon, I noticed that lightning was only in one faraway corner and the thunder sounded like distant bongos. Even Darby's hiccups had gone away.

"We need to head back," Dawn said.

Robbie nodded. "This might be our chance. For all we know, there could be another wave of storms headed toward us."

We stood as best as we could and clambered back out onto the hill. Some of us were rubbing our necks and some of us were shaking out our legs. I had no idea how long we'd been hunkered on the ledge, but it was long enough to feel stiff and sore.

"My side hurts from being mushed up against the wall," I said, massaging my shoulder.

"My foot's asleep," Darby muttered as she hobbled along beside me.

"My rear end went numb," Dawn said, walking kind of straight legged.

For a moment or two, we stretched and wiped our eyes and breathed in the damp, electric-smelling air. I even did a couple of cartwheels to loosen up my limbs and get out some trapped wiggles.

"So what now?" Darby asked.

"Let's see what the creek looks like," Jay suggested.

We all walked to the ridge where we'd first noticed the flooding creek and bent down to have a peek. The water had gone down, but was still higher than before and running fast. The wooden bridge was there, only it was lopsided, and half of it — the half that led to our side of the creek — had collapsed.

"Aw, man," Nelson grumbled.

"Guess we can't go out the way we came in," Jay said.

"What's the plan?" Robbie asked.

"Why don't we go one way and you guys go another way," Dawn said, pacing about and tapping her chin. "Hopefully, one of us will find a safe place to cross."

Jay and Nelson exchanged glances and shook their heads. "No way," Jay said. "You guys will try to finish the game."

"What?" I'd forgotten all about the game. It seemed so unimportant now.

"Come on, we're past this," Dawn said. She held out her palm toward Jay. "Truce?"

Instead of taking her hand, Jay folded his arms across his chest. "Why should we trust you? You already stole Robbie."

"We didn't steal Robbie," I said, "he came to us."

Nelson made a face at Robbie. "And now he can tell you all of our secrets."

"What secrets?" Robbie said, throwing up his hands. "We don't have any."

"You'll take them to our flag," Nelson said.

Robbie looked shocked. "I told you I didn't help them. She explained it."

"But now you've changed sides," Jay said. "What's stopping you now?"

"Everyone needs to calm down!" Darby shouted.

I was tired and hungry and wanted to get moving again. But everyone was just standing around fighting. It made my pent-up jitters come back.

I tried squeezing my eyes shut and pressing my hands over my ears, but I could still hear all the shouting.

"You just want to win the game!"

"I don't care about the game!"

"We had an agreement!"

"I'm tired!"

I tried humming to help drown out the racket.

"You changed sides!"

"You guys didn't believe in me!"

I tried dancing around while humming.

"I just want to eat!"

"Aunt Jane's going to be worried!"

Finally, I couldn't take it anymore. "Stop yelling!" I yelled. "Everybody just stop yelling!" Only it didn't do any good. Everyone was making noise and no one was listening.

Suddenly, I became aware of another voice — one that sounded kind of faraway. I brought my hands down and listened. Somebody was calling out, "Hey! Yoo-hoo! Over here!"

While the others kept squabbling, I glanced around for the distant shouting person. "Look!" I cried out. I pointed a few yards away where Dawn was standing rather majestically atop a big rock, her hair blowing back in the breeze. She had pulled the boys' flag out of the backpack and was holding it above her head with both hands.

Nelson sucked in his breath. Jay mumbled, "Oh no."

"What is she doing?" I asked Darby. Darby just shrugged.

"Hear me!" she cried.

Everyone fell silent.

"This competition ends now!" she hollered, shaking the flag. Then she leaped off the boulder and started running down the hill.

CHAPTER THIRTY-ONE

De-Escalation

Dawn

I ran as fast as I could, clutching the flag in my hands.

Pounding noises behind me let me know that the others were in pursuit. Good. I wanted them to follow. As long as they didn't try to stop me, everything was going according to plan.

Eventually, I made it to the bottom of the ridge. I was out of breath, but I wasn't done yet. I glanced back and forth, searching for just the right spot. Over on my right, a flat slab of limestone stuck out about a few feet above the water.

Perfect.

When the others reached the bottom of the hill, I was standing on the slab.

"Dawn, what in tarnation?" Delaney yelled.

Darby held up her hands. "Be careful!"

My sisters seemed like they were about to cry — they were in such a panic. The boys looked worried, too. Nelson had run so hard down the hill he'd tripped and slid the last yard. He lay there, gazing up at me with wide, wondering eyes.

"Now hear this," I shouted. "I'm throwing in the towel — or the flag, as the case might be. And this time I don't care if you boys call us quitters. This game is over." With that, I tossed their flag into the water below. The current caught it and swirled it downstream.

I watched it bob out of sight, then carefully climbed down.

"So you did have our flag," Jay said matter-of-factly.

I shrugged. "It doesn't matter. The only thing that's important is us getting home before dark."

"But . . . why?" Robbie asked. "You could have won."

"We're all in the same mess right now. I had to do something that would help all of us — not just me and my sisters," I explained. "That dang competition was ruining everything."

Darby patted me on the back. "You did the right thing."

"Yay! It's over!" whooped Delaney, bouncing up and down. I knew just how she felt. I'd never been so happy to be a loser.

Jay didn't say anything. He just blew out his breath and raked his fingers through his dark wavy hair. Then he strode over to where Nelson was sprawled on the ground.

"Here," he said, bending down and holding out his hand. "Let me help you up."

Nelson took hold and started scrabbling upright. "So does this mean we automatically — *ow!*"

"What's wrong?" Jay asked.

"I think I — *ow!*" Nelson yowled. "I hurt my foot. I can't stand up!" He fell back on the grass, grabbing his right leg.

"Aw, man. Now what are we going to do?" Robbie asked. "It's starting to get dark."

"You and I can carry him," Jay said.

"The whole way?" Robbie stared in the direction of camp. "But it's pretty far and the ground is all muddy and slippery."

"Maybe we can go get help and send it back to you guys," Darby suggested.

"Don't leave me here!" Nelson cried, tears dripping down his face. "More bad weather might come. Or wild animals. Or ghosts!"

Suddenly, an ear-splitting noise emanated from the nearby brush.

Nelson shrieked. "See?" He flopped onto his side and curled into a ball.

"What was that?" Jay asked, backing away from the direction the sound came from.

"I know what it is!" Delaney bounced merrily. "Come on out, boy! Here, boy."

Sure enough, Mo came crashing through the brush, his nostrils flaring, ears twitching, and mouth chomping on some kind of grass.

"How the heck did Mo get over here?" Darby asked.

Delaney shrugged. "No idea."

"Maybe he followed you Delaney," I said. "He really likes you."

"Aww. Were you looking for me? I'm so glad you didn't drown, Mo." Delaney patted his forehead.

"You sure he's tame?" Nelson asked, unfurling slightly.

"Of course," Delaney said.

"Don't let him get too close and stomp me." Nelson eyed Mo's big hooves warily.

I knew exactly how Nelson felt, and it made me feel even sorrier for him. "This just happens to be the world's most incredible donkey. He's so gentle, you can ride him. So if you don't want to stay out here in the dark, you should let us put you on his back."

"Wait a sec," Jay said. "Remember how you guys knew where our flag was? How you noticed the limestone gunk on the shoes?"

I nodded, unsure why he was bringing that up again.

"Well, look at the donkey's feet."

We looked. Mo's hooves were halfway covered in mud and grime.

"So?" I said, unsure what he was getting at.

"So he probably left tracks, right? And maybe the tracks will lead us back to where he crossed the creek."

"Hey! That's a great idea!" Delaney said, clapping her hands.

Jay and Robbie carefully lifted Nelson and put him on Mo. Then we followed the half-moon shaped indentions back in the direction of camp. Darby and Robbie were in front, keeping an eye out for donkey tracks. After them came Delaney, who led Mo with Nelson lying along his back. Jay and I took up the rear.

Except for Delaney cooing at Mo, no one talked much. Daylight was starting to fade, and I wondered if they were just as worried as I was that we wouldn't make it back in time. Plus, things were still a bit awkward after all that arguing.

Jay kept opening his mouth as if he were going to say something, but then seemed to change his mind. Finally, he turned toward me and said, "What you did back there. Giving up the flag. I don't think I would have ever done it — and that bugs me."

"Why wouldn't you have?"

"I guess I'm too proud. I just always want to be top dog." He shook his head. "See, Nelson is all outdoorsy and athletic. He plays soccer back home and is really great at it. And Robbie is talented at sketching and painting. The only thing I'm good at is leadership."

"I'm the same way — kind of a lot," I said. "But . . . being a good leader doesn't mean you always have to be in charge."

Jay gave me a confused look.

I tapped my chin and tried to think of the right words. "Power is good — and it feels great — but it's more important to make sure everyone works together," I said. "Like the difference between being a dictator and being president."

"Right," he said, nodding slowly.

We didn't talk for a long time after that. Everyone concentrated on trudging through the brush. The path seemed to be fairly smooth, and it stayed close to the water's edge. But I wondered how long it would go. The sun was gone and the air was turning chilly — and it felt even chillier because we were so wet.

At one point, just as the sky was turning the purple shade of dusk, Darby came to a stop.

"What's wrong?" I asked.

She glanced back and smiled. "Look," she said, pointing up.

It was the rope swing — the same one I'd fallen off of the first day. It was still hanging from the limb of the big live oak on the opposite bank.

"Um . . . that won't help us," Robbie said. "It's far away on the other side. And kind of dangerous looking."

"But it means we're close," Darby said.

"Also" — I turned and smiled back at Jay, who was walking alongside Mo — "look near the top of it."

Just below the knots holding the swing to the tree was a white pillowcase with a design on it. Our flag.

"You don't need it now. You guys already won," I said. "So can we just leave it up there? Proof through the night that the Brewsters were here camping?"

Jay grinned. "Sure."

"We haven't made it through yet," Darby said.

"We will," I said. The sight of the flag gave me hope. It looked proud up there, wavering in the breeze. A testament to our bravery.

We kept on, pushing through the bushes and weeds. Delaney chattered to Mo, Nelson whimpered, and Jay mumbled encouraging "It's okays" to his littlest brother.

"You guys, I don't know what to do," said the shape of Robbie in front of me. "I can't find anymore tracks."

"Me either," came Darby's voice.

"We're close, though," I said. "I just know it."

As we rounded the next bend, the path seemed to disappear. Not only could we not see tracks, we were having a hard time seeing anything but brambles. Everyone came to a full stop.

"What do we do now?" Robbie asked, his voice shaky.

"I know," Darby said. "Delaney, try and yell for help. Maybe we can get someone's attention."

"Okay." Delaney stood facing the creek and cupped her hands over her mouth. "Hello-o? Hello-o? Can anyone hear me?" she shouted over the sounds of rushing water.

We stood very still waiting.

"Hello-o?" Delaney tried again.

"Hello?" came a voice — it sounded far, but not too far. "Is someone out there?"

I squinted across the water and could just make out a stooped figure standing on the other side, wearing a wide-brimmed fishing hat: Mr. Bartholomew!

"Yes! It's us!" Delaney called back. "Dawn, Darby, and Delaney Brewster! We're lost on the other side and it's dark!"

"I've got a flashlight here. Can you see it?" A beam of light shot out from where Mr. Bartholomew stood. He aimed it forward and suddenly, I could see the reflection of the water, the line of the opposite bank, and, nearby, a raised road that connected our side to that side.

The old causeway! The scene of our fishing challenge loss. I never thought I'd be this glad to see it again.

The lake below was rushing faster, but the causeway was clear. I wondered if that was where Mo had trotted across.

"Yes! We see it!" I called back. "Please keep shining that light. We're going to cross over."

"Take it easy going across!" Mr. Bartholomew shouted. "It might be slippery."

The causeway was fairly wide, but it was dark and the only light was the beam of a distant flashlight. As we stood on the bank, waiting to cross, Darby started humming a soft, slowed-down version of "When the Saints Go Marching In." I joined in, and then, little by little, so did the others.

First, Darby and Robbie headed out onto the causeway. As they crossed, they took measured, sure-footed steps in time with the music. Next went Delaney, coaxing along Mo with Nelson on his back. Jay and I followed a safe distance behind.

"You're doing fine," went Mr. Bartholomew. "Not too fast now."

I saw Darby and Robbie make it to the other side and breathed a grateful sigh. Then Delaney, Mo, and Nelson stepped down off the causeway, and I made a little happy noise.

Finally, my foot hit wet grass, and I felt a sparkly rush of relief. I hugged my sisters. I thanked Mr. Bartholomew. I even kissed Mo on the nose.

"Yes!" I shouted. "I love camping!"

CHAPTER THIRTY-TWO

Fireside Chat

Darby

Thank heavens," Aunt Jane cried out as we walked into HQ with Mr. Bartholomew. She ran over and grabbed all three of us in one big hug. I ended up smooshed into Delaney's hair, but I didn't mind. I was happy to be back at camp and extra happy to see Aunt Jane.

A bearded man in long plaid shorts ran over to Jay, Robbie, and Nelson. He hugged each of them gently and helped Nelson limp over to a nearby bench. I figured he must have been their dad. Mr. Moyers wore the same watery-eyed expression that Aunt Jane had for us.

"Are you kids okay?" Mrs. Kimbro asked, rushing out from behind the counter. She had a phone in one hand and a map in the other. "We've been so worried! We were just gathering up a search party."

"We're fine," Dawn said. "We all pulled together and made it back."

"Mo helped, too!" Delaney said.

"Goodness, you all must be chilled to the bone. Have a seat near the fire." Mrs. Kimbro ushered us toward the fireplace, which crackled and glowed irresistibly. "I'll get marshmallows and skewers."

Mr. Bartholomew found a couple of big blankets. He draped one over me, Dawn, and Delaney, and the other over Jay and Robbie. In the meantime, Aunt Jane took a look at Nelson's foot and had him wiggle it. I heard her tell his dad that it was probably a sprained ankle.

"If that's the worst that happened, then we're lucky," said Mr. Moyers.

"Darn tootin'," said Dawn. "Camping is serious stuff."

"That's why you need rules and guidelines," Delaney said.

"And friends," I said. Robbie smiled at me and I smiled back.

"And donkeys!" Delaney added.

Mrs. Kimbro came back with marshmallows, chocolate, graham crackers, and long metal skewers, and we related our adventure as we made s'mores. I was so hungry, I didn't even mind the marshmallows.

We told everyone about the sudden storm, how we found shelter underneath the rocky ledge, and how Mo had led us back and Mr. Bartholomew had guided us with his flashlight. We didn't mention the arguing or spying or how Robbie left his group to join us. All that seemed so silly now.

Occasionally, one of the boys spoke up. Nelson talked

about how we'd helped him when he got hurt, and Robbie mentioned Presidential Trivia and how it helped us not be scared. For a long time, Jay just sat there under his blanket, not saying anything.

Later, during a lull when we were all chewing our food, Jay stood and said in a scratchy voice, "It was my fault. I got us all into that mess. I'm sorry."

"It's not your fault," I said. "It's nobody's fault."

He shook his head. "You guys tried to stop the competition, but I didn't listen. I was stubborn. I'm sorry I got carried away. And Nelson, I'm sorry you ended up hurt because of it. And Robbie" — Jay paused, his voice quivering — "I was really unfair to you. I owe you an extra apology on top of the other apology."

He turned toward his brother and held out his hand. For a few seconds Robbie just looked into his eyes. Then he grinned. I felt a lump in my throat as they shook on it.

"But Jay, you also helped save us," I said. "You're the one who had the idea about following Mo's tracks."

"And I have to admit, you really know how to shake up an opponent," Dawn said.

"See?" Delaney said. "You must be pretty incredible, Jay. Because Dawn doesn't say nice things to people unless she really means them."

One side of Jay's mouth tugged upward. He seemed to be feeling better.

I popped the last bit of chocolate into my mouth and stood to face Jay, Robbie, and Nelson. Then I raised my hand in a salute. Dawn and Delaney did the same.

This time Jay smiled for real. He brushed cracker crumbs off his hands and saluted us back. Robbie followed suit, and Nelson saluted from his bench.

"I must say, this is the most civilized of campgrounds," Mr. Bartholomew said. Then he saluted, too.

We hung around for a while longer, enjoying the fire, eating more food, and visiting with everyone. I didn't talk much. I was enjoying sitting in my chair and listening to the happy sounds around me.

To my left, Mr. Moyers was explaining to Mrs. Kimbro how he cooks fish. To my right, Aunt Jane was telling Jay about her days playing basketball. In front of me, Dawn was playing Go Fish with Nelson. Behind me, Mr. Bartholomew was telling Robbie and Delaney about the donkeys they used when he served in the Army, and Delaney told him that she someday wanted to get a paint horse. "I think I'll name him S'mores," she added.

I felt warm and snug, but not just because of the fire and gooey treats. Something amazing had happened here, the type of thing that changes your whole view — as if the whole world had tilted a little to the left.

In the past, we've helped family, friends, and even strangers, but this was the first time we'd banded together with adversaries. It was hard at first — and then it wasn't bad at all, at least once we realized we weren't that different. Maybe all enemies are just people you don't understand yet?

I wanted to ponder that some more, but my mind felt slow and dreamy. As I yawned I saw Aunt Jane notice me.

"I better get these girls back to the trailer for some dry clothes and a good sleep," she said, getting to her feet.

"I'll never take those two things for granted again in my life," Dawn said.

Dawn, Delaney, and I said good-bye to everyone, thanked Mr. Bartholomew, and told Nelson we hoped he healed up quickly. Then we straggled toward the exit.

"Thanks for everything, Tammy," Aunt Jane said as we started heading out the door. "I'll come back early tomorrow to help figure out the storm damage."

"No hurry, Jane. You see to those girls. There will be plenty of opportunity. After all, we'll be seeing a lot of each other."

Because I was zonked, it took a while for that last part to sink in.

"What did Mrs. Kimbro mean?" I asked Aunt Jane as we crunched down the gravel path. "Are we going to come camping again soon?"

"Sort of," she said. She stopped walking and turned to face us. "Well, I guess now is as good a time as any to tell you all. I've decided I'm going to go into the camping business."

"You . . . what?" Dawn asked.

"Tammy really needs some help or she's going to have to sell, and I'd hate to see this place go. Plus, I think I'm ready to leave Boston. I feel like I've done all I can do there and, as I mentioned already, I sure do hate being far away from family."

"But do you know how to run a whole campground?" Delaney asked.

"Well, I know how to run an establishment where people come to get away from it all. I know some things about camping and horses and outdoor sports. I think I could be good for this place, just like it was good for me all those years."

"Wait . . ." My sleepy brain was slowly processing, deciphering each word and phrase. "Does this mean you'll be moving back to Texas? That you won't be so far away anymore?"

Aunt Jane grinned so big, I could see it in the dark. "That's exactly what it means."

Once again we ended up in a big group hug and once again I was mushed up against someone's ear or nose, but it didn't matter. I was so happy, I could be jabbed with cactus prickles and still feel great.

"Of course you'll be good for the campground," Dawn said.

"Just like you're good for us," Delaney said.

"It needs you, Aunt Jane," I said. "And so do we."

Dear Mom and Dad,

Mrs. Kimbro, who runs Lake Lewis Campground, is letting me borrow her computer. I wanted to send a quick email to let you know that everything is fine. You might have received some distressing letters or postcards by now, and I know I was a little bit reluctant to go on this trip. I just didn't want you to be worried.

When we get home we'll tell you all about our stay here. And Aunt Jane has some news of her own. But in the meantime, I just wanted to say thank you for forcing me to come here against my will.

Love,

Dawn

CHAPTER THIRTY-THREE

This Land Was Made for You and Me

Delaney

I knocked on the door of the Moyers' RV and took a step back. There was muffled music in the background and I heard some thumping sounds. Then Mr. Moyers opened the door and smiled at me. He was wearing a tie-dyed shirt and his long hair was in a tidy braid.

"Good morning, Delaney," he said. "Want to come inside and watch cartoons?"

I had to think about that one for a moment. "No, thank you," I said at last. "I have people waiting for me. I just came to get Robbie."

"He's finishing up. Won't be long now," he said. "So did you get some good rest last night after your adventures?"

I nodded. "Sure did. Darby said I kept talking about clowns, but I don't remember."

"Hi!" Robbie popped into the door frame, next to his dad. He was holding a paper bag and was grinning real big.

I grinned back. "Hey there. Everyone's in the Neutral Zone. They sent me to get you."

"I'm ready." He looked over at his dad. "I'll be back soon with the others."

"Don't take too long. We need to leave in an hour if we're going to make it home by dinnertime."

"All right."

"And Roberto? No tests of endurance or treks into the wilderness, okay?" Mr. Moyers winked at us.

"We won't," Robbie said a little sheepishly. "Sorry," he said to me after the door shut.

"No problem. Dawn says stuff like that to Darby all the time."

Mo was standing near the path to the Neutral Zone. I ran up and hugged him around his neck.

"I think he came to say good-bye," I said to Robbie. "He knows you're leaving."

Robbie patted him on the neck. "I'll miss you, Mo. You saved us, you know. You and your big feet."

"I'm going to miss him, too, when we leave tomorrow," I said sadly, pressing my forehead against his muzzle. "But I'll probably get a chance to see him again. Now that Aunt Jane will be helping to run this campground, Dawn wants us to come back every spring break. Like a tradition!"

"That's nice. Maybe we'll come back, too," Robbie said. "I'll ask Dad."

"That would be stupendous! We'll have a reunion."

Robbie turned and saluted Mo. "Democrat the Donkey, aka 'Mo,' you are the bravest donkey that ever existed."

"And the sweetest. And cutest. And the most loyal," I added, patting Mo's back.

We left him chewing on a leafy bush and poked our way through the brush until we came into the clearing, where Dawn, Darby, Jay, and Nelson were waiting for us. Nelson was sitting in a lawn chair Jay had carried out, but the others were standing.

"Finally," Dawn said. "We were going to get Mr. Bartholomew and his flashlight to help find you."

"Ha-ha. Very funny," I said, rolling my eyes.

Robbie went and stood by his brothers and I lined up with Dawn and Darby. For a few seconds we just hung around smiling awkwardly at one another.

Eventually, I cleared my voice and said, "We sure are sorry you guys have to go."

"Yeah," Dawn said. "Just when we started liking you."

"Plus, we could use your support. We're organizing a camp cleanup," Darby added.

We had just brainstormed it a little while ago after breakfast and Morning Cartwheels. Aunt Jane had mentioned how the storm left behind lots of debris and broken stuff all over the campground and we offered to go around picking it up — safely and in a group. When Mr. Bartholomew stopped by to check on us, he said he'd help, too.

"Sorry we'll miss that," Jay said.

"Yeah," Nelson said.

"We're leaving tomorrow," I said. "Which is weird. In a way it doesn't seem like we've been here a week already, but it also seems like we've been here a long long long time."

"Yeah," Robbie said. "Seems that way to me, too."

It got quiet again.

"So anyway . . . we got you a present," Nelson said. "Go ahead and give it to them, Jay."

"A present?" Dawn said.

Jay nodded and smiled that unreadable smile of his. Then he reached into his backpack and pulled out a folded cloth, which he handed to Dawn.

"It's a flag. Another one," he explained. "We felt you guys should have it because, well, you guys were the real winners."

Dawn looked confused. "But I forfeited."

Jay shook his head. "You put aside personal glory for the good of the group," he said. "You are the better leader. You guys governed best."

"Go ahead and look at it," Nelson urged.

Dawn held it up by the edge and let it unfold, and Darby and I leaned in to look. Sure enough, it was their original design, only a couple of things were different. This time, there were six hands holding on to each other at the wrist, making a hexagon shape. And the words across the top read "United in Friendship and Fun."

"Wow," I exclaimed. "That's beautiful."

"Plus we made you guys zucchini bread," Robbie said. He stepped forward and handed me the paper bag. I peeked inside and saw a plastic container. A wonderful smell hit my nose.

"Thanks, you guys," I said and passed it to Darby.

"That's very thoughtful," Darby said and passed it to Dawn.

"I feel a little lousy because we didn't bring you guys anything," Dawn said.

Robbie laughed. "That's okay. We wanted to do this."

"Besides," Jay said. "You guys have already done lots for us."

We all stood and grinned at one another. No one spoke for a while, but it wasn't a squirmy silence. It was nice and friendly.

Eventually, Robbie said they had to get going so we followed them back to their RV. It was kind of slow because of Nelson. I was glad he seemed able to get around better. And he had found a big stick that he leaned on as he walked. He told us that he and his dad would carve cool things into it.

Once we got to their camper, we stood in a line and saluted them. They saluted back. Then they all climbed inside and shouted good-bye — Mr. Moyers, too. We waved as the RV pulled out of the campsite, and I ran in circles with the flag held over my head.

"I never thought I'd say this, but I'm sorry to see those charlatans leave," Dawn said.

"Me too," Darby said.

"Me three," I said.

We decided to take the road to HQ instead of the dirt path so that we could walk arm in arm. It was one of those beautiful, sparkly days that makes it seem like Mother Nature is showing off. Birds sang and flitted about. Wildflowers waved at us in the breeze. I just knew this would be one of those memories that got blown up big and framed inside my mind — me walking with my sisters after our big adventure.

"So, Dawn," I asked as we headed toward HQ, our arms linked together so that we made a short chain. "Are you still okay to run against Jay for president?"

"Sure," she said. "Although I'm hoping I won't have to."

"You're hoping he's changed his mind about running?" Darby asked.

Dawn shook her head. "I'm thinking that even though he's a great opponent, he'll make an even better running mate."

ACKNOWLEDGMENTS

Writing, like camping, can be a messy, wondrous, sometimes scary, and often joy-filled test of endurance. I could not have gotten through this project without guidance from many terrific people.

Huge thanks go to Erin Black, David Levithan, Yaffa Jaskoll, Brooke Shearouse, Antonio Gonzalez, Lizette Serrano, Emily Heddleson, Melissa Schirmer, and the entire team at Scholastic.

Erin Murphy, you are my flashlight beacon. Forever thanks go to you, Dennis Stephens, Tara Gonzalez, Kirsten Cappy, and all the other great minds at EMLA.

Help with research came in many forms. Biggest thanks goes to my father, Jim Ford, who started taking me camping and fishing as soon as I could walk. Other key help and encouragement came from Cynthia Leitich Smith, Nikki Loftin, Becka Oliver, Beth Sample, Clare Dunkle, Gillian Redfearn, Samantha Clark, Kendall Miller, Tony Burnett,

Jordan Smith, and all my fellow writers with Austin SCBWI and the Writers' League of Texas.

This story is, in many ways, an amalgam of past camping adventures. For those key memories, I must thank Esther Ford, Amanda Ford, Jason Ford, Renee Ziegler, Fletcher Barton, Owen Ziegler, and Sage Barton; extended family who gathered at Silver Bay YMCA in 2016, including Nancy Moore, Joe T. Moore, Charles Bush, Judy Bush, Bob Lewis, Helen Lewis, T. Ann Nolan, E. A. Nolan, Laura Bush, Justin Bush, Harmony Huntington, David Carnahan, Tim Barton, Sidney Barton, Carolyn Carcasi, and various offspring and grandoffspring; and the Quiet Hill Ranch gang, including Alvaro Rodriguez, Mike Guentzel, Susan LaRonde, Courtney Havenwood, Jay Landers, Owen and Jodi Egerton, Jim and Cindy Whatley, the creature alternately known as Donny the Donkey and Hank Williams IV, and all the children, hooligans, and critters involved in those campouts.

One nice thing about writing a series is that I can include names that I accidentally left out of previous acknowledgments. Thank you, Gerald and Charlotte Barton, for sharing tales that led to a key aha! moment.

With this endeavor, as with everything, huge credit goes to my husband for his patience, keen insight, and mad sandwich-making skills. Thank you, Chris. I love this adventure we're on.

And finally, extra special thanks goes to the Kimbro family. I love you, Tammy. Sparkle on.

ABOUT THE AUTHOR

Like the Brewster triplets, **Jennifer Ziegler** is a native Texan and a lover of family, history, barbecue, and loyal dogs. Although she only has one sister, she does know what it is like to have four kids living in the same house. She is the author of *Revenge of the Flower Girls* and *Revenge of the Angels*, as well as books for older readers, including *Sass & Serendipity* and *How Not to Be Popular*. Jennifer lives in Austin, Texas, with her husband, author Chris Barton, and their four children.